The Uist Girl Series Book 3

SONS AND BROTHERS

A captivating family saga novel set in Scotland

MARION MACDONALD

Photographs for front cover are from Canva

For my siblings
Willie, John, and Catherine

and

In Memory of my husband's grandfather,
Jimmy McAneny, who walked to London in the
1936 Hunger March.

A brother is a friend God gave you; A friend is a brother your heart chose.

Unknown

CHARACTERS

The Macdonald Family

Chrissie Macdonald	Our Heroine
Roderick Macdonald	Her husband (Deceased)
Roddy Macdonald	Son of Chrissie & Roderick
Donald Donaldson	Son of Heather & Colin
Heather Macdonald 1 (deceased)	Daughter of Roderick & Lily (deceased)
Heather Macdonald 2	Daughter of Bunty & Johnny

The MacIntosh Family

Marion MacIntosh	Chrissie's mother
Angus MacIntosh	Chrissie's father
Johnny MacIntosh	Chrissie's brother
Lachlan MacIntosh (deceased)	Chrissie's brother
Morag MacIntosh/Hamilton	Chrissie's sister

The Adams/Hepworth Family

Mary Hepworth	Bunty's daughter
Bunty Adams/Hepworth	Mary's mother
James Adams (deceased)	Bunty's Father
Frederick Adams(deceased)	Bunty's stepfather
Grace Adams	Bunty's mother
Harry Hepworth (deceased)	Bunty's husband
Charles Adams	Bunty's brother

Other Characters

Sir Arthur	The Laird
Colin Donaldson	Former Factor and Donald's
(deceased)	father
Victoria Donaldson	Colin's Sister
Janet McLeod	Johnny's Wife
Aunt Katie	Angus's Sister
Maude	Solicitor/friend of Aunt Katie
Michael Hamilton	Morag's husband
Mr Abernethy	Island Solicitor
Murdo Mackenzie	The Postman
Ian and Sarah Fraser	Postmaster and wife
Findlay Simpson	New postmaster
Archie Campbell	Roddy's school friend
Flora McIntyre	Roddy's school friend
Cynthia Walters	Mary's school friend
Jimmy Thompson	Roddy and Donald's landlord
Annie Thompson	His wife
Rosemary Thompson	His daughter
Theresa Dunlop	Roddy's girlfriend
Patrick Dunlop	Her father
Hector McDougall	Headmaster at Portree HS
Professor Nicholson	Guidance Professor at GU
Professor Harley	Roddy's Law Tutor
David Lamont	Doctor at Royal Hospital
Moira Munro	Housekeeper
Deirdre MacFarlane	Sister Tutor
Elizabeth Crawford	Sister on Men's Medical

GAELIC WORDS USED IN THIS BOOK

I'm not a Gaelic speaker but have used some words to indicate when characters are speaking in Gaelic. My apologies if I have used any of them incorrectly.

Athair	Father
Ciamar a tha thu?	How are you?
Leanabh	Baby
Machair	Low-lying coastal grazing land
Mamaidh	Mummy
Mathair	Mother
Mo graidh	My darling
Seanair	Grandfather
Seanmhair	Grandmother

THE MEANS TEST

People who lost their jobs depended on unemployment benefit, otherwise known as the dole. A man without work was entitled to benefit from the unemployment insurance scheme for the first six months after he became unemployed.

However, to cut costs, the government introduced the Means Test in 1931. Officials visited families to assess whether they were entitled to help. This involved finding out how much the families earned or possessed.

To qualify for dole, a worker had to pass the Means Test, and the sum paid to each family would be based on this test. Families with some savings or a small additional income, found their dole was reduced. The officials who carried out these tests were often seen as insensitive, and many families were offended.

The test created many problems for families. Tensions were caused because, if an older child had some work, or a mother had a part-time job, or a grandparent was living in the house without paying rent, the Means Test could result in dole being refused. Heirlooms and items such as pianos had to be sold, and savings spent before the dole was received.

This led to the hunger marches that are referred to in this novel, which were organised by the National Unemployed Workers Union.

PROLOGUE

Helensburgh, Scotland, 1935

I feel like a character in one of thon new Agatha Christie mysteries where all the characters end up in the same place and Inspector Poirot is called in to solve a murder. I pray to God there won't be one of those. It's the day of Donald and Mary's wedding and everyone who was part of our lives back in 1923, apart from Johnny, is here at my sister Morag's hotel in Helensburgh. When Bunty Hepworth told Mary she intended coming home for her marriage to Donald, she felt it would be unfair to her mother for them to marry in North Uist. Although it means my father and our friends can't be here, it's easier for everyone else. But I can't help feeling a little sad that none of our friends from North Uist are here; that it isn't the Reverend Macaulay performing the marriage ceremony, and that we will sing the hymns in English instead of Gaelic.

I wasn't sure how I would feel seeing Bunty Hepworth again after all these years and I had mixed emotions when I did. She arrived yesterday with her mother and her brother, Charles. She looked the same, yet different. Older, I suppose, and a little forlorn. I felt something akin to pity for her, and yet it's me who will lose everything I hold dear if she finds out the truth about Heather. Helensburgh is the place where I first set eyes on my Heather. I'll never forget when Charles handed her over and left her with me. She was a beautiful two-week-old baby, whose eyes had barely opened, but whose sucking reflex was already in evidence. When she turned and nuzzled into me, hoping for some milk, how I had longed to put her to my breast. But my milk had never come in after I had miscarried, so I needed to use a bottle. It reminded me of when Donald was born, and I had to feed him after his mother died. Love for this little person, who I was now responsible for, had overwhelmed me and I promised her I would always look after her. Even then her hair was black and wild, just like Johnny's and I was

1

worried people might guess the truth, but they never had. I hoped to God that Bunty wouldn't either.

When my mother and I arrive at the church, there's no sign of the wedding party. I wonder where Donald and Roddy have got to. They should be here by now. I hope nothing is wrong. Roddy was really upset last night, and I think I know why. I hope Donald hasn't guessed. But it's not just them I'm worried about. Heather is Mary's bridesmaid, so she's coming to the church in the car with Mary, Charles, and Bunty. What if, somehow, Bunty has realised that Heather is her daughter and has run away with her? My stomach turns to mush, and I think I'm going to be sick. As I try to decide what to do, my thoughts go back to 1923, the year they had all left the island.

1923

LEAVING

CHAPTER ONE

I cried when Donald and Roddy left the island. They had been my life and my link to Roderick. What would I do without them? Cradling Heather in my arms, I let my tears flow freely. It was selfish, I know, to burden my sons with my tears, but I couldn't help it. The last few months had been so harsh. My emotions seemed to bubble up at the least thing, and I found it difficult to keep control of them. The act of deceiving people into thinking Heather was my baby had been all-consuming. I hadn't considered what my boys leaving the island would mean to me or to them. But as I waved goodbye, I knew it was the end of my role as their mother and the beginning of their journeys into adulthood. I wondered where those journeys would take them.

As the boat left the harbour, I put Heather in her pram and began my walk back to the croft. Although I would still be a mother to this little girl in the pram, I wondered which roads my journey would take me on. Murdo interrupted my thoughts, and I was glad of the respite from my overthinking.

'Chrissie, wait up. I'm just taking the mail to the post office. I'll walk with you.'

He was pushing a cart with several sacks of mail in it.

'Hello Murdo. How are you?'

'Och, I'm fine Chrissie, but what about you? I couldn't help noticing you shedding a few tears there when your boys were leaving. Such a sad situation you've had to deal with these last few months.'

I could feel tears welling up again. I wished people wouldn't be kind. It only made me weak, and I needed to be strong.

'It's been hard, Murdo, but I have my lovely wee lassie to keep me going. Is there any mail for the croft, do you know?'

'No, sorry I don't. Mr Fraser will need to sort it out. Are you expecting something, then?'

'Well, we've heard nothing from Johnny since he left. Do you know if Janet has written to her mother yet?'

4

'Not that I know of,' he told me, just as we reached the post office. 'Well, that's me. I'll take my leave of you now, Chrissie. Enjoy your walk. If there's anything for you from Canada, I'll be sure to bring it up to the croft tomorrow.'

It was a beautiful late summer day and there were crops in the field ready for harvesting, but I couldn't help sighing as I said goodbye to Murdo. It was six months since Johnny and Janet had gone to Canada and neither my mother nor Janet's mother had received any word telling them where they had settled. They still didn't know about Roderick or about Heather. Others in our community had heard from their loved ones, so we knew they hadn't been lost at sea. My worry was that Johnny and Janet's relationship had been affected by him finding out Bunty was pregnant, and they had gone their separate ways. Not hearing from them, however, had offered me respite from having to decide whether to let Johnny know I had his baby. My mother and father thought I should, as it would set his mind at rest. But what about my mind? What if he came back for Heather? What would I do? How could I survive without my little girl? I loved her like my own.

CHAPTER TWO

His mother cried like all the other mothers who stood on Lochmaddy pier waving their children off to school. But Roddy wondered just how sad his mother really was to see him go, now that she had a new baby. Sometimes he felt he was last on her list of priorities. She had gone away for three months and left him and Donald to cope on their own after their father died. As if she was the only person who was sad about losing Daddy. And look at what had happened with that Mrs Hepworth. She had thought it was his fault when he failed his first test, but it was only because she had deliberately marked him down.

He was with Archie Campbell and Flora McIntyre. Archie wasn't as bright as him and had only got through the qualifying exam with some extra help from him. But they were both glad of it, as he and Archie were best friends. They enjoyed each other's company and had a good laugh together. Archie was a head taller than him and what you call lanky. All skin and bone and kind of caved in at the shoulders as if he were trying to hide how tall he was. He had a huge Adam's apple that bobbed up and down when he was excited about something, and he became excited often. He preferred running around outside to sitting down and doing his homework and stared out of the window a lot when the teacher was giving them their lessons. The teacher was always telling him to stop dreaming.

He was a dreamer, too, but his dreams involved getting a good job and becoming wealthy. The only way he knew how to do this was to work hard and do well at school. He always paid attention to what the teacher said and did his homework. Before he died, his father had told him he was confident Roddy would make a success of his life, so he didn't want to let him down. Besides, he was sure he was looking down on him from heaven, like a kind of guardian angel, and would see everything he was up to.

He wasn't so happy about Flora McIntyre going along, though. She had been one of the children who had spread the gossip about

Roddy's father being a murderer and about Donald's mother being a Red Indian. Archie didn't bother about these things. It was something Roddy liked about him, but it was strange given that his mother was the biggest gossip on North Uist. Flora was a pretty girl, with curly brown hair falling below her shoulders that she liked to swing from side to side as she walked. He noticed she was getting little buds on her chest, which she liked to stick out whenever she chatted to the boys.

The crossing over to Skye was uneventful, and when they arrived, someone called Mr McDougall herded them together like a flock of sheep. It turned out his full name was Hector McDougall, and he was the headmaster at Portree High School. It was Mr McDougall who taught him about debating. However, at that time, he wasn't sure about him. He hated people in authority because of how Bunty Hepworth had treated him at Lochmaddy Primary. It had soured his feelings for anyone who was a teacher and trusted none of them because of that experience. During term time, the children would stay in dormitories or if they had relatives, they would stay with them. The boys' dormitory was right next to the school, but the girls' accommodation was in the town. The teachers obviously didn't want the boys and girls to be too close to each other. When he and Archie found out they were to be billeted together, they gave each other the thumbs up. If you had to leave home, it was good to have a friend to share a room with.

CHAPTER THREE

Murdo arrived one morning not long after I had met him in Lochmaddy with a letter from Canada.

'Here it is, Chrissie. A letter for your *Mathair* from Canada. Is it your Johnny's handwriting?'

'Yes. It is. Thanks, Murdo. I'll let you know what his news is when I see you next.'

Mother was out collecting eggs, so I left the letter on the table for her while I fed Heather. I loved the soft snuffling sounds she made while she sucked on the bottle teat. Her little legs kicked enthusiastically, and the milk ran down her wee chin when she let it slip out, trying to catch her breath. Her eyes, our Johnny's eyes, looked up at me totally trusting as she latched on to the teat again. I hadn't got into a routine with her yet and it sometimes made her grumpy, but today she was good as gold. Looking after a baby felt new to me after such a long time, but I was up for the challenge. I would need to balance it with helping on the croft, so my mother and I would share her care. When she came in, my mother's cheeks were pink from the fresh wind blowing outside and she smiled widely at us.

'How's my granddaughter getting on?'

'She's managing just fine, *Mathair*. I'll get you a cup of tea when I've finished feeding her. There's a letter on the table from Canada. I think it's from Johnny.'

We looked at each other. A letter from Johnny meant I would need to decide if I was going to tell him about Heather.

'At long last. I hope it's good news.'

She opened the letter eagerly while I winded Heather, then put her down for a nap. I filled the kettle and put it to heat on the range, then spooned the tea into the pot ready for when the water boiled. While she sat reading, I watched her face, trying to guess from her changing expressions what the letter said. She had never been too good at the reading, so it took her a while to get through it all. I mashed the tea and then poured it to stop myself from snatching

8

it from her and reading it myself. At last, she put the letter down and took a gulp of her tea.

'Well. Don't keep me in suspense.'

'He's in America.'

'America?'

'Yes. He's got a job in a car factory in Detroit, and Janet has a job in the hospital there. They're renting a house with a garden and think that is where they'll settle permanently.'

'Does he mention anything about Bunty or the baby?'

'No. Why would he? He doesn't know we know about it.'

'Are they happy? Does he sound happy?'

'Read it for yourself and see what you think.'

I read his letter, taking in all that he said on paper but trying to read between the lines. They had had a shaky start, he wrote, but were now settled in Detroit. What the shaky start was, he didn't say, but I was sure it was related to the news Bunty had given him just before he sailed. It was ironic that he had settled in an industrial city and yet had refused to move to Glasgow. But, he told me, he was learning new skills, and Janet was in a great place to advance her career. He reassured us he and Janet were happy with their new life, and when they made their fortune, they would come back for a visit someday. He finished by apologising for not writing earlier and begged us to write to him soon with all the news from home.

'Well, what are you going to do, Chrissie? Will you tell him about Heather?'

'Do you think he's truly happy, *Mathair*? If I thought he was, I wouldn't say anything about Heather, as it would mean he had moved on with his life.'

'I'm not sure. I'm surprised he's gone to live in a city, so I think he's only doing it to make Janet happy. Because of the guilt he carries, I think he would do anything for her.'

I agreed, so perhaps I should tell him the truth. How I wish we had a telephone, and I could talk to him. Writing letters was so slow and you couldn't say everything you wanted to.

9

CHAPTER FOUR

Donald waved to Chrissie as the ferry left Lochmaddy, taking him to a new life with his Aunt Victoria. Sir Arthur was travelling with him. It had been his decision to remove him from North Uist because of all the scandal about his parentage and about Roderick. He was glad to get away as his only friend was Mary and she had left several months ago to live with her grandmother in Manchester. The last few months had been hard, as Mammy had gone to live in Helensburgh with Aunt Morag because she was sad about Daddy dying. Life was just one bad thing after another. Although he was glad to get away from North Uist, he was dreading going to a new school where he would be the new boy. He felt sick at the thought that they might find out about him.

When his mother asked to talk to him the day before he left, he felt uneasy. She was always trying to explain things, and sometimes she frightened him when she talked so seriously.

'Donald, I know the last couple of years have been hard for you, and I'm sorry. I shall miss you so much when you leave, but you know there's nothing I can do about it, don't you?'

He nodded and bit his nails as he waited for her to continue.

'I want to tell you a bit more about your *mamaidh* and about her *mamaidh*.'

What else did he still have to know? Wasn't there enough?

'As you know, Heather Macdonald was your mother, but we still don't know for definite that her father was James Adams. Scientists are doing work to create a test that can give a definite answer, but I think it's a long way off. So, you will need to decide for yourself who you would prefer to be your grandfather.'

So, he had to choose between a man who had left his family, was a drunk, and tried to kill Roderick, or a man who buried that man's body to cover up his death and took his Indian squaw wife to live with him. Not much of a choice. As if she had read his mind, Chrissie continued.

10

'I can see you think it's like Hobson's choice, but remember, it was Roderick who gave Lily and Heather a home and looked after them. And he loved you like his own son, just as I do.'

He could see tears in her eyes and momentarily wanted to run into her arms and feel the warmth of her body against his. She was his *mamaidh*, after all. But he was now ten and she would be his *mamaidh* no longer, so he had to get used to living without her.

'There's something else you need to know, Donald.'

What now? He couldn't take much more.

'Lily's surname before she married James Adams was Norwest, not Waskatamwi, which we put on Heather's birth certificate. Waskatamwi is Cree for Lily. I think it's important you know this in case you ever decide to find out more about your family on your mother's side.'

He looked at Chrissie in disbelief. Did she really think he wanted everyone to know about Heather and Lily? He wanted to bury it deep and never think about it again.

CHAPTER FIVE

After waving goodbye to her mother, Mary was happy. The Long Island Poor House seemed to have worked some kind of magic on her. She appeared much calmer than the last time she had seen her and, despite trying hard, she could not get that image out of her mind. It was the day of Uncle Roderick's funeral, and her mother had what the doctor called a breakdown. She was talking to Uncle Johnny and seemed convinced that he was talking to her, even though he was in Canada. But things got worse when they arrived home. Her mother told her she needed to have a hot bath, and she made Mary help her fill the tin bath with boiling water from the kettle and pots on the stove. She could never wipe out the image of her mother lying in that bath with a knife in her hand. It had been such a relief when Mrs McIver and Dr McInnes arrived. Her mother tried to fight them off, but Dr McInnes put a needle in her arm, and she became unconscious.

It had been a hard couple of weeks for her after her mother went to the asylum. She stayed overnight with Dr McInnes and then moved to the croft, where Auntie Chrissie was staying with Roddy and Donald. Auntie Chrissie seemed in a world of her own and went out walking alone several times a day. Donald had been lovely to her, but Roddy ignored her most of the time. She didn't really blame him, as her mother had done terrible things to his family. So, when her Uncle Charles turned up and told her he would take her home to Manchester, she was relieved. She longed to see her grandmother again as she had missed her so much these last few years.

Life felt strange when she moved back to Manchester. After the quietness of North Uist, Manchester was noisy and dirty. But she loved being back with her grandma, so that was some compensation.

'Why didn't you write to me, Grandma? I thought I'd done something wrong when I didn't hear from you.'

She could see Grandma hesitating and then she said.

'I'm sorry about that, Mary. I didn't know where you and your mother had gone, but as soon as I did, I wrote to you. Didn't you get my letter?'

'No. Maybe it got lost in the post.'

'Maybe. Anyway, you're back here now and I can't tell you how glad I am that you are.'

She grasped Mary in a fierce hug, then looked at her earnestly. 'Don't you ever think you have done anything wrong. Nothing that has happened is your fault. Your mummy is ill, and that's why she did what she did.'

'Donald and I will write to each other, Grandma. He and I are best friends.'

'That's nice for you, chook.'

'When will Mummy come back and live with us?'

'I'm not sure, but not for a few months, anyway. I think you'll have started school by then.'

School had been difficult at first. Most girls had already formed friendships, so being new to the school made it difficult to join them, and her Scottish lilt didn't help. She was teased mercilessly at first about it, but gradually, as she acclimatised and spoke like the other girls, they accepted her as one of them. It was to be another year before she saw her mother and by then she was a stranger to her.

CHAPTER SIX

A few weeks after the letter from Johnny to my mother arrived, another letter arrived, this time addressed to me. Murdo was curious.

'Two letters from your brother in as many weeks, Chrissie. He must have a lot to tell you.'

'Well, he needs to make up for not writing to us for six months, Murdo,' I laughed. 'It was my mother's turn a few weeks ago, so it's mine now.'

He nodded, and I went inside, tearing the letter open as I did so.

Dear Chrissie

I hope this letter finds you well. I'm sorry I haven't written sooner, but things have been difficult between Janet and me since we arrived in Canada. We nearly split up when I hit the bottle. You could see how upset I was when we left Uist, but it wasn't because I was leaving home. It was because Bunty told me she was going to have my baby. I can't tell you how bad I felt about that. I hated the thought that I had taken advantage of her and left her literally holding the baby. But I dreaded to think what would happen to my child with a mother as unstable as Bunty seems to be. It filled my head the whole way to Canada, and I must confess I was very unkind to Janet. I hardly spoke to her, I drank constantly, and I got into fights.

When I ended up in a police cell in Canada, that sobered me up and I knew I couldn't go on the way I was doing. So, I confessed everything to Janet; told her about my relationship with Bunty and about the child she was carrying. She was very upset to begin with and refused to talk to me. She said she needed time to think about what I had told her. But eventually she agreed to give our marriage a chance, so long as I gave up the drink and didn't try to find Bunty or the baby. I've agreed to that, and we have moved to Detroit, where there is plenty of work for me and for her. She deserves the chance to make a career in nursing and I need to support her.

14

I expect you're wondering why I'm telling you all this. It's because I want to find out what happened to my baby. I didn't mention it in my letter to Mathair as I don't want to upset her and Athair. I know they would be upset to think they have a grandchild they will never see. But for my peace of mind, I need to know, and I hope you will do what you can to help me. As you and Bunty were friends, I'm thinking you might know what has become of her and the baby. Chrissie, I hope you don't think badly of me. I'm a weak human being, but I don't think I'm a bad one. I can't tell Janet as it would finish us, so if you find out anything, could you write to me at the PO Box on this letter? It will be for the best.

Please send my love to Roderick and the boys. Roddy will head to school in Portree this year, won't he? I hope all goes well for him. He's a clever lad and will go far, I'm sure.
Your loving brother
Johnny

By the end of the letter, I was in tears.

'What's wrong Chrissie? What's he saying?' asked Mother.

I passed his letter over to her to let her see for herself.

'Och *Mathair*, it's not so much what he's said, it's that he doesn't know all that's happened to our family since he went to Canada.'

So much had happened since Johnny left. Roderick was dead, the doctor had locked Bunty up in the asylum, and her brother had given me her baby to look after.

'What are you going to do, Chrissie? Will you tell him the truth?'

'Yes, I will, *Mathair*. It would be cruel not to. My news would set Johnny's mind at rest, and it would give him and Janet a better chance of making a go of their marriage.'

I knew I was doing the right thing for Johnny and Janet by telling him I had Heather, and hoped I was doing the right thing for Heather and me. So long as Johnny kept my secret, all would be well.

15

CHAPTER SEVEN

Donald liked his Aunt Victoria. She was kind, and they shared a love of reading. She had a small library in her house, but she sometimes took him to the local public library, which was full of all kinds of books on all kinds of subjects. It was a magic place. He would have spent all his time there if Aunt Victoria had let him. Reading was an escape from the world and real life. When he read, he could be anything he wanted to be, and it was his love of reading that made him want to be a writer when he grew up. When he told his aunt, she bought him a leather-bound writing journal and told him he should start now and not wait until he grew up. It was the best present he ever received and wrote in it every day.

Aunt Victoria was what was called an invalid. She had difficulty walking and had callipers on her legs. She often told him how much she enjoyed having him around the house to help her when she needed it. A nurse helped her, but it wasn't the same as having her nephew, she told him. He was sure that was the reason she sent him to a local day school despite what the Laird had said. He had held his breath when he heard the Laird telling her he would be better off at boarding school as it would toughen him up. What a relief when she stood her ground and said no. He enjoyed going home every day and knew he would have hated boarding.

He didn't make any close friends, however, as he kept himself to himself. He did what was necessary to be accepted. But he invited no one home, as his aunt suggested he should, and he accepted no invitations to visit any of the other boys in his group. To satisfy the curiosity of the teachers and the other children about this new boy who spoke with a funny accent, he told them a version of the truth. He told them his mother had died when he was born, his father had died of the flu, and his aunt was now his guardian. No need for them to know any more than that.

When he turned twelve, his contented life with his aunt changed. She could no longer keep him at home with her. It was a condition of the trust his father had set up that he must go to the same boarding school in Edinburgh that his father had gone to. His old fear of people finding out about his heritage returned, and he withdrew into his shell again. The teachers and boys he met there tried to befriend him, but when he didn't respond to their friendly overtures, they gradually left him to his own devices. The most enjoyable thing about his school years was what he learned about literature. He spent much of his time in his room, reading whatever his English teacher suggested and writing in his journal. But he also loved climbing Arthur's Seat and sitting in the meadows reading on a fine summer day. So, his only friend was still Mary, who wrote to him faithfully every month. She was a shining light in the darkness of his life.

CHAPTER EIGHT

I can't believe how quickly the last few years have flown past. Heather is starting school and I'm having a photograph of her taken so that I can send a copy to Johnny. I wrote to him back in 1923 at the PO Box number he sent to me telling him I had his daughter. I wasn't sure whether I was doing the right thing and, I must say, I had a wobbly moment when he wrote back, saying he longed to see her and wished he could come home. But fortunately for me, he didn't want to upset Janet. He wrote saying she would never forgive him if she found out he had written to me, trying to find out what had happened to Bunty and the baby.

I can't tell you how happy I am that you have my little girl. I was so worried she might still be with Bunty and might be in danger because of that woman's mad behaviour. Thank God she was in the asylum and couldn't have a say about what happened to the child. You did well to convince her brother to let you have Heather, and you seem to have fooled everyone into believing she is yours. Janet's mother was telling her all about Heather in the last letter she sent. I am so sorry to hear about Roderick and about you losing your baby. You've had a hell of a time of it since we left Uist, but I can tell from your letter that little Heather has brought you a lot of joy. I want to come home and see her, but of course I can't tell Janet that you have Heather. I promised her I would never try to find Bunty or the baby and if she knew I had written to you, she would be hurt and angry. I've put her through so much I don't think she would ever forgive me for letting her down again.

Since then, every few months, I have written to him to let him know how she is doing. I still send everything to the PO Box. I feel bad at deceiving my old friend, but she and Johnny seem to have settled in well to living in Detroit and I don't want to do anything to endanger their marriage. Johnny works in a motor producing factory, which pays good wages and Janet is now a ward sister in the city hospital. He says they've even invested in the company he works for by buying some shares. Apparently, everyone over there is buying stocks and shares, so he thought he would do it too. He will make much more money with investments than by just putting his money in the bank, he says. I don't really know what stocks and shares are, but Roderick always just kept his money in the bank and that's what I'm doing.

Starting school is a big milestone in a child's life, so that's why I'm having the photograph taken. I'm going to get one of Roddy too, while he is up here working on the croft for the summer and one of us all together. The photographer duly arrived and set up his equipment, while we all put on our best clothes. He took one of Roddy, one of Heather, and then one of the three of us with my mother and father. When the photographs arrived a few weeks later, I was very pleased at how smart we all looked. I paid particular attention to Heather's photograph to see if there was anything of Bunty in her, but I couldn't see it. I was busy wrapping Heather's photograph when Roddy came in for a cup of tea. He and my father had been out picking turnips. I put it aside and poured him a cup and gave him some oatcakes and crowdie, then got on with what I was doing.

'Is that the photograph of Heather you've got there? Who are you sending it to?' he asked, munching on his snack.

I paused in my task, feeling awkward. Did Roddy suspect something?

'I'm sending it to Johnny,' I said warily. 'He likes me to send news of you both.'

'Well, why don't you send the one of me too? That way, he'll get to see what a handsome bloke I've grown into.'

'Och Roddy, you're such a big head. You'll need to learn some humility,' I laughed with relief.

'How is Johnny? Are he and Janet enjoying life in America? I bet he gets a shock when he sees Heather's photograph. She's his spitting image.'

I grew cold at his words. Did Heather look so much like him? Just as well, I was sending the photograph to the PO Box and not to their home address. If what Roddy said was true, then Janet might suspect the truth when she saw the picture of Heather.

'Do you think Heather looks so like Johnny? I know she has his hair, but can't you see a bit of me in her?'

'To be honest *Mathair,* no, I can't. Anyway, I better be getting back outside. *Seanair* will wonder where I am.'

And off he went, oblivious to the consternation he had caused me.

CHAPTER NINE

Mary was sometimes afraid of her mother and worried that she might become ill again. She kept going on about a baby and about going to Canada to find the father. But she had never had a baby, and the only person she knew in Canada was Uncle Johnny. But he had married someone else, so she didn't think her mother could have had a baby with him. When her mother talked like that to her, her grandma stepped in and stopped her, but this led to tension between them. When Mary was twelve, her mother announced that she was going to Canada to see where her father, James Adams, had lived. Mary was terrified she would want her to go too and was relieved when she said she was going on her own.

'I don't want to leave you, Mary. You know how much I love you, don't you?' she said, stroking Mary's face gently. 'But your Grandma and Uncle Charles have made me see it wouldn't be fair to take you away to Canada when you're just beginning your secondary education.'

'I understand Mummy. I love you too. Will you write to me and tell me all about where your father lived?'

'I will, my darling.'

Although she didn't like to admit it, life without her mother was much easier. She didn't have the constant nagging fear in her belly that her mother would become ill again. Also, there were no arguments any longer between her mother and grandmother about her. She had sometimes felt like piggy in the middle when they argued about what was best for her. The main thing they argued about was her education. Her mother wanted her to go to boarding school, but her Grandma had argued against it. She thought it would be bad for Mary to have to leave home so soon after just coming back. Eventually, her mother agreed she could go to a private school for girls in Manchester that was within easy reach of where they lived.

By the time she got to secondary school, Mary was interested in music, fashion, and going to the pictures. So she had much in common with her classmates, especially her best friend Cynthia Walters. Cynthia's hair was as dark as Mary's was fair, but they shared the same blue eyes. She was curvy and liked to do her hair like the stars they watched at the pictures and was interested in the latest fashions. Mary still missed Donald though and wrote to him every month, telling him what she had been up to and how she was getting on at school. He faithfully wrote back to her, but sometimes she became upset as he sounded so unhappy.

When it was time for Mary to leave school, she decided she wanted to train as a nurse. It was something that suited her personality. She was a caring person and enjoyed looking after people. When she went for the interview, however, the Matron who interviewed her made it clear she would need to be much more than a caring person. A strong stomach and being hard working were the attributes she would need to become a successful nurse. The Matron had not misled her, as she found out when she began her training, but at the time she was more preoccupied with what being a nurse could teach her than the actual work of nursing. The sicknesses people got in both their minds and their bodies interested her. She told herself learning about the mind and the body would help her deal better with her mother if she ever returned home and had another breakdown. But, the truth was, she was worried about her own health. She didn't want to become like her mother and wanted to find out as much as possible so she could prevent it from happening.

Her mother seldom wrote to her and her Grandma now. After finding her father's grave, she had taken the vacant post of schoolmistress in Saltcoats. This was the town where her father was killed and where people still remembered Chrissie and Roderick. She never mentioned Johnny or her health in her letters, so Mary assumed she had come to her senses and given up the notion that she had had a baby with Johnny. She hoped so.

CHAPTER TEN

Roddy lost his virginity in his third year at Portree High School with, to his surprise, Flora McIntyre. He discovered she was getting bullied by two boys who shared the dorm with him and Archie and had told them to leave her alone. They ignored him, of course, so he had to show them he was serious. Knowing that causing trouble in school might get them expelled, they all walked out one day to the foot of Fingal's Hill to fight. They were unlikely to be caught there. It was a fist fight, and he beat both boys hands down. Archie went with him, so he felt like one of those heroes he had read about who challenge their rival to a duel and they fight at dawn for the love of their life. He was fighting for Flora as she came from North Uist, not because she was the love of his life. He wasn't going to let some bullies from Berneray give her a hard time.

She somehow found out what he had done, and after that, she followed him about like a lovesick puppy. It was she who kissed him for the first time and then his hormones kicked in and the inevitable happened. It wasn't great the first time, as she was a virgin, and he didn't want to hurt her. But she insisted they did it again so she could get used to it and it would have been rude to refuse. It wasn't always easy for them to meet because of how the dormitories were set up, but the woods were nearby and on warm afternoons, they could sneak out and have fun. So, he had a splendid time in his last year at Portree High School. Few of the boys had girls fancying them the way Flora fancied him.

Despite the distraction offered by Flora, he passed all his exams with flying colours and Glasgow University offered him a place to read law. It delighted his mother when he told her. Heather was six and at Lochmaddy Primary School, where he and Donald had gone. He hoped she was having a much better time with her teacher than he had. She was a cheeky wee thing, so his mother still had her hands full with her and with her share of the work on the croft. He thought she probably missed him being at home, as she couldn't see what he was up to, and perhaps it was just as

23

well. He noticed her sniffing his clothes when he came home, hoping to catch him out and give him a telling off for smoking the cigarettes. But she needn't have worried. Although he and Archie had tried it, only Archie had taken to buying cigarettes with his pocket money. Roddy preferred to save his money and besides, Flora had told him she didn't like the smell of it on his breath when she kissed him. And he enjoyed her kisses too much to give them up for cigarettes.

When it was time for them to leave school, he told Flora he was intending to go to Glasgow rather than go home. He thought she looked disappointed, but she was very sweet. She promised to write to him every week, but he knew he wouldn't answer. He had plans that didn't include the likes of Flora McIntyre. Even so, he was glad when she wrote to him not long after he arrived in Glasgow to tell him she had a new boyfriend, and she was sorry to let him down. Although he had enjoyed his relationship with Flora, he wouldn't miss her, as he had too much to look forward to.

He would miss Mr McDougall, though. Their friendship had begun after his first term, when he and Archie had taken up shinty. They had never played it before, but they both engaged in the game enthusiastically and became star players for the school team. As Mr McDougall was a big fan of shinty, he gave them some coaching in his spare time. After the coaching sessions, he would invite them up to his house for tea. It was part of the school block, so close to the boys' accommodation. Archie never went, but Roddy enjoyed it. Mrs McDougall always had home-made scones or cakes and as a hungry teenage boy, he got stuck in. He found it relaxing sitting with them. The wireless was always playing in the background while Mr McDougall supped on his pipe and Mrs McDougall knitted. It was a real home from home for him and he would never forget their kindness.

24

1929

LIVING AND LOVING

CHAPTER ELEVEN

Heather started school a year ago and Roddy is going to the Glasgow University in October. Roderick would be so proud of him as he's the first in either of our families to go on to higher education. I feel so sad when I think of everything Roderick is missing out on, but I believe he is looking down on us and can see that we are managing as best we can without him. Roddy is home for the summer and is helping my father on the croft until he is ready to go to Glasgow in October. Tomorrow, we will go to see Mr Abernethy, the Solicitor, to talk about the trust deed Roderick set up for Roddy's education. After that, we will go to the post office to set up an account for him so that he can receive his monthly allowance from the trust. We are so lucky that Roderick was canny with his money.

Donald has come up for the school holidays too. He has only been back to Uist twice in the past six years, so I'm delighted that I'll have my two boys for the summer. Donald has told me he plans to go to Glasgow University too when he finishes school in two years' time, which I'm glad about. Hopefully, the boys will rekindle the old friendship they used to have before Colin Donaldson turned our world upside down. Although they have completely different personalities - Roddy is outgoing and confident, while Donald is lacking in confidence and finds it difficult to be in company - both have turned into fine-looking young men. I had hoped Donald would grow in confidence once he was away from Uist and the gossips, but it appears he has not.

Now that Heather is at school, I'm back working in the post office. Although I love helping on the croft and being a mother, it is good to do something more. Last year was a wonderful year for the Rural and we celebrated women getting the vote on the same basis as men with a big open-air celebration at the market stance. It was such good fun but after it was over, I stepped down as chairwoman. Elizabeth Macaulay, the Minister's wife, took on the role so I don't have the same involvement as I used to. The opportunity to get the job in the post office came up when Ian and

26

Sarah Fraser moved back to the mainland. When Sarah found she was expecting a baby, she wanted to be nearer to her family. Who can blame her, with a sourpuss of a husband like Ian Fraser? Anyway, the Post Office appointed a new postmaster by the name of Findlay Simpson, Fin, for short. He's a widower with two teenage girls, who live in Glasgow with their grandparents. He was looking for a housekeeper and a part-time post office assistant, so I applied for the latter and got the job because of my previous experience.

I'm not sure what I think of Fin. He is very focussed on his job and doesn't talk much, so although I've been working with him for six months now, I hardly know anything about him. Mairi Campbell got the job as his housekeeper, and she says the same. She takes after her mother and likes a good gossip so is disappointed that she hasn't much to report on the Findlay Simpson front. I only know he's a widower and has two daughters because I asked him straight out if his wife wasn't with him because North Uist was so remote. You can imagine how sorry I felt when he told me his wife was dead, but it explained a lot. Perhaps I would be sad and withdrawn too, if I didn't have Heather.

CHAPTER TWELVE

Roddy could barely repress his excitement as he made his way along University Avenue to meet his tutor. He had signed up for politics and law. It was October, the beginning of a new term and a new life for him. His tall figure carried the tweed suit he wore well, and he knew he cut a fine figure. He had been a member of the debating group at Portree High School and had discovered a talent for public speaking. The Headmaster, Mr McDougall, had suggested politics after a heated debate on the merits of land reform.

'You would make a grand politician, Roddy. Eloquent, handsome, and just a little self-centred.'

It was a backhanded compliment, but he had taken it. From that time forward, he set his mind on doing whatever it would take to become a lawyer and then, if it was in God's plan for him, a politician. The more he thought about it, the more it made sense. He could make a difference in politics. The Western Isles constituency had voted in the same party every time, and nothing ever changed. Most of the politicians who stood were part of the ruling classes and knew nothing of what living as a crofter meant. Not that he himself knew that much about it. But he had spent time on his grandfather's croft during the holidays and helped him look after the sheep and collected the peat. It still annoyed his grandfather that not enough land was given to local people after the war, despite the promises the government had made.

It had been worth living in that hostel in Portree for all those years away from his family, apart from holidays, to get the opportunity he now had. He knew it had been hard on his mother, losing his father and him, but having Heather had helped fill the void. He had easily passed the entrance exam and won a bursary to allow him to complete the education that would enable him to go to university. No thanks to that witch, Bunty Hepworth, who had done everything she could to make him fail. But today was not a day for sadness and regret. It was a day of new beginnings and the possibility of adventure.

As he walked through the quadrangles, imagining the other famous sons of Glasgow University, he felt honoured to become one of them. He knew Donald would follow him to university, as Colin Donaldson had planned it from the time he claimed Donald as his son. But he was here first. He had done something on his own merits, not because he had money or a title. He knocked on the oak-panelled door and waited until he heard a voice telling him to enter. His stomach turned to water, and he thought he was going to be sick. This was it. The person who would make or break his first year at university. He opened the door and confidently walked through to disguise his nervousness. The room was full of shadows and dust motes floated in the sunshine streaming through the window. It smelled of musty books and the familiar pipe tobacco that Mr McDougall used to smoke. It took him a moment to notice a man sitting behind an enormous desk covered with books and he became flustered. However, the man stood up immediately, holding out his hand in greeting, and his next words helped Roddy to relax.

'You must be Roddy Macdonald. I've heard a lot about you from Mr McDougall at Portree High School. He and I used to play shinty together.'

What a coincidence that he knew Mr McDougall. As he thought about his headmaster, he smiled. He would miss him. He had become a father figure to him while he was at the High School and knew he had been lucky that he saw something in him and wanted to nurture it. Hopefully, this man would feel the same.

'You are from the islands, sir?'

'I am indeed. Broadford in Skye is where my family comes from. Couldn't wait to leave and yet I go back every year and feel nostalgic for my childhood.'

Roddy didn't believe he would ever feel nostalgic for his childhood. It had been one of difficulties; too many. Although he loved his mother, as a son should, she irritated him. She was always giving her attention somewhere else, and he felt second best. Even although Donald wasn't her son, he used to feel he got

29

all her attention. She felt sorry for him being an orphan, but she never grasped what a big deal it was for him to find out that she and his father were not Donald's parents. He was always worried that they would come in one day and tell him they weren't his parents, either.

Professor Nicholson stood up and shook Roddy's hand over the desk. He was as short as Roddy was tall and had a full head of white hair and a bushy, grey beard. His olive-coloured eyes were bright and mischievous, and Roddy immediately liked him. He felt himself relax and just knew everything was going to work out. Professor Nicholson would be his Guidance Tutor, so it would be to him he would go if he had any problems. Hopefully, there wouldn't be any, but Roddy knew life was unpredictable. You never knew what was round the corner as he had found out to his cost in his younger life.

For the first couple of years he spent in Glasgow, he took advantage of his newfound freedom. He joined several clubs, including the debating society and the University's motorcycle club. Fortunately, the money his father left had allowed him to buy a motorcycle. The adrenaline rush of navigating the tight, meandering roads of Loch Lomond on the weekends was something he loved. The companionship of his fellow students in the club was a bonus. It was there he met most of the people he would spend his days at university with. Most of them had gone to a private school like Donald, but they didn't hold it against him. It was something he liked about those with privilege. So long as you appeared to be one of them, they accepted you. It was only when the stakes were down that they would stick together and exclude you from their circle. But he only found this out when he met Theresa Dunlop in his third year at university.

CHAPTER THIRTEEN

In his second year, Roddy moved into digs. He decided living with Katie and Maude clipped his wings. It was okay in his first year when he was green behind the ears, but he felt he now knew the lie of the land at University. He had made friends and was enjoying himself. He liked to smoke and drink in moderation and those were two things he couldn't do with his aunt and her friend looking on. At first, he enjoyed living with them. There were always meetings, and it gave him more of an understanding of the political issues going on in the world. It was they who introduced him to his new landlord, Jimmy Thompson, and his wife, Annie. Jimmy was a member of the Communist Party and a staunch supporter of women's rights, so that was how they knew him. He and Annie had a flat in Partick and took in lodgers to make ends meet. Jimmy had been a teacher before the war but couldn't work now as he had lost a leg during combat in France. Annie worked as a telephonist.

The flat was a good size. It had a bathroom and a kitchen. The kitchen was the hub of the house and was where Jimmy and Annie had their meals and listened to the wireless. It was also where Jimmy and Roddy spent many nights arguing the pros and cons of Communism versus Socialism. Roddy was now a member of the Labour Party and although they agreed on many things, there was still a lot to argue about. The flat had three other rooms. There was one for Jimmy and Annie, one for when their daughter Rosemary came home for a visit and one spare room. This room had two single beds in it and was the one they rented out to Roddy. They encouraged him to find someone to share with, to help him with the rent, but Roddy wasn't keen on that idea. He could afford the rent from the allowance he received, so he didn't bother getting someone else in. It was only when Donald told him Glasgow University had accepted him to study literature that he asked Jimmy if his brother could share with him.

Living with Donald would help to heal the breach that had grown between them. He was ashamed when he remembered how cruel he had been to him when they were children and often thought of the slippering his father had given him. He had deserved every slap he received with that slipper, but it had left him humiliated and probably still a little resentful of Donald. Of course, Bunty Hepworth had taken advantage of the rift in their relationship. She deliberately tried to make matters worse between them. First, by only inviting Donald to play with her daughter Mary and then causing problems for him by marking him down in his schoolwork. It was just one more thing that had led to him being jealous of Donald. He remembered how much he resented Donald's family connection to the Laird, as he thought it meant his future was secure. But look how things had turned out. Nothing in life was certain. Donald wasn't much better off than him now because of the Wall Street Crash and the Depression was hitting people hard. Too many had no work and were forced to rely on unemployment benefit.

Donald was quiet in comparison with himself and never argued with anyone. So far as he could tell from his letters, he still rarely socialised. Roddy suspected it was because he didn't like to get too close to people in case they found out he was of mixed race. He had taken it badly when Bunty Hepworth had spread that rumour about his mother being a Red Indian, and it used to rile Roddy that he never stood up for himself. He was always getting into fights while Donald would just stand and cry when Flora McIntyre and others tormented him. The last time he had seen him in Uist, he still bit his nails, the way he did when he was a child. Roddy hoped University life would suit him and he would make friends. To help him with that, he had signed him up for a Fresher's weekend in Balmaha on Loch Lomond. He himself had gone to something similar when he began university and had made loads of friends. Hopefully, it would be the same for Donald.

CHAPTER FOURTEEN

Donald wasn't due to begin University until October, but he moved in with Roddy at Jimmy Thompson's flat in the summer when the school term finished. They shared a room, and it was there he re-discovered the friendship he had enjoyed with his brother in the early years before Colin Donaldson showed up. After the self-imposed lonely years he had spent at school in Glasgow and in Edinburgh, he appreciated his brother's company. Roddy led an exciting life and was always encouraging Donald to go to the pub, the dancing, or the pictures with him and sometimes he went. He wondered if Roddy still got involved in these activities when it was term time. When he started university this year, he would probably only study. Not just because he wasn't particularly used to socialising, but because he thought he wasn't as bright as Roddy.

Roddy always seemed to have girls interested in him wherever they went, and he took full advantage of their interest. He was never without a girlfriend or a partner to go dancing with or to the pictures. The postman had delivered a letter from Mary that morning telling him she was coming to Glasgow next year to do her nurses' training. So, life seemed bright with possibilities at the thought of being re-united with his childhood friend. Although he didn't envisage that she could ever be his girlfriend, he thought it would be nice to spend time with a girl.

After he received the letter, he had gone out for a walk. When he arrived home, Jimmy was hovering at the door. It was a lovely summer evening, and he was taking the air. Because of his leg, he couldn't walk very far. Normally, Donald tried to avoid him, as he was a bit of a bore. He either talked about the war or about politics, neither of which interested Donald particularly. But tonight, he was in a good mood because of Mary's letter, and he agreed to have a cup of tea with Jimmy when he offered it. Of course, the first thing he mentioned was political.

'What do you think of this Means Test the government is putting us through?'

'If I'm being honest, Jimmy, I don't really know much about it. I'm not on any kind of benefit, so it doesn't affect me.'

After he said the words, Donald realised how crass he had been. Jimmy obviously depended on benefits to help him now that he couldn't work because of his war injury. But surely he must receive a pension which wouldn't be means tested.

'Maybe you could explain it to me,' he said quickly, to cover up his insensitivity.

Jimmy was only too willing to explain, so Donald sat supping his tea while Jimmy explained, hoping not to be too bored.

'Well, Donald, there are many people in Britain who are unemployed now because of the Depression. Too many of those people are in the West of Scotland and other areas of the UK which relied on traditional industries, such as coal, iron, and shipbuilding.'

He took a gulp of his tea and then continued.

'Until this year, unemployed men could claim benefit and it didn't matter what other household income they had. But that all changed when the National Government introduced the dirty Means Test.'

'Why do you call it 'dirty' Jimmy? Surely, if people don't need the unemployment benefit because perhaps they're like me and have other income, they shouldn't get it.'

Jimmy laughed, but not with humour.

'Well son, there's few people like yourself trying to claim unemployment benefit. I'm afraid it's people who are already poor and hungry that need to claim it.'

Donald felt foolish.

'Why do you think hunger marches are taking place all over Britain?'

'I didn't know there was.'

'Don't you read the papers, lad?'

'No, I prefer reading poetry or a novel.'

Jimmy got up and limped over to a sideboard next to the fireplace, and came back with a newspaper, which he handed to Donald.

'Read this, son. It'll enlighten you more than any of that poetry or the novels you read just now.'

Donald looked down at the newspaper called *The Daily Worker.*

'Thank you Jimmy. I'll read it tonight.'

As Donald was getting ready for bed, he realised he had got a lot out of Jimmy's explanation of the Means Test and was curious about the newspaper he had given him. No doubt Jimmy was hoping he might turn him into a Communist like himself, but Donald doubted very much that would happen. But after he read the D*aily Worker,* it made him realise how much he missed by just reading literature. From now on, he resolved to take a daily paper and keep up to date with what was happening in the world.

CHAPTER FIFTEEN

On Donald's first day at university, he woke up early. For a moment, he forgot what day it was, then his usual anxiety kicked in. Roddy was lying in the bed opposite to him, still asleep. He let out a deep sigh, hoping to disperse the fluttering moths in his stomach. Roddy stirred, stretched, and rolled onto his side to face him.

'Not feeling nervous, are you, brother?'

'A bit, if I'm honest. I hate going into new situations.'

'Try not to worry. I'll be there by your side. Let's meet for lunch and you can tell me how you get on.'

He nodded, glad Roddy was walking with him today. The comfort of having his brother with him on his first day at University was as welcome as it had been all those years ago, on his first day at Lochmaddy primary.

It was a grey, misty October day, and the leaves were changing colour but hadn't begun falling on the pavements yet. The smoky smell of autumn heralded in the new season, and he wondered what this new stage of his life would bring. He knew he and Roddy made an incongruent pair as they walked up University Avenue to the lofty gates of learning. Roddy was tall and well-dressed in a tailormade suit, while he was slightly shorter and dressed in casual clothes of tweed and wool. They didn't look like brothers, and of course they weren't, but he felt like they were.

Roddy, unsurprisingly, was enjoying being the big brother, the one who knew the ropes and would show them to him. He didn't mind. He was glad to have him on his side. As they walked alongside the scores of young men and women like himself, he could almost taste their excitement and fear and realised he wasn't alone. Somehow that feeling took away his dread, and he looked forward to what the day would bring.

Once he matriculated, he made his way to meet his tutor. A dislike developed between them almost immediately. Professor Hobson was a tall, gaunt man with pince-nez spectacles that he peered over when Donald entered the room. He didn't beat about the bush, but immediately asked him what his reading interests were.

'Come in, young man, take a seat. I'm Professor Hobson. Tell me, what kind of things have you been reading?'

Donald thought he might have asked him something about himself, but he didn't. The professor was only interested in what he had read. This suited him, as he didn't need to tell him the usual half-truths about his background.

'I've read traditional novelist like Dickens and Hardy, some of the American novelists and I have also read D H Lawrence. I was sorry to read about his death earlier this year. I've also taken to reading a daily newspaper after my landlord gave me the Daily Worker to read.'

'Your reading will help you do well on this course, but I would guard against reading the Daily Worker. It's a communist newspaper.'

'Have you read it yourself, sir?'

'No. I wouldn't touch it with a barge pole. Stick to the Glasgow Herald or the Daily Mail.'

The professor's attitude annoyed him, but he said nothing. It was his first day, and he didn't want to start off on the wrong foot.

However, at the stands introducing new students to the various clubs and societies on offer, he paused at the Young Socialists one. Without knowing, his professor had encouraged him to do the very thing he objected to. Surely, it was important to people in the teaching professions to have an open mind. Hadn't the authorities tried to ban Lawrence's genius because it didn't conform to their views? Well, he would let no one stop him from finding out more about socialism. It didn't mean he would become a Communist. It only meant he was willing to listen to other people's points of view, and he thought that was a good thing.

He went along to Balmaha, to the weekend high jinks that Roddy had signed him up for, but as usual he felt out of place. There was a lot of drinking, dancing and raucous activities that just didn't appeal to him. But the one good thing that came from it was

37

he met the editor of the Gilmorehill Globe, the student newspaper. He invited him along to the Union any afternoon to have a chat about joining the editorial board of the newspaper, which he did. It was to set him in good stead, when Rosemary Thompson suggested he write an article for the Daily Worker a year later.

CHAPTER SIXTEEN

It was because of him that Roddy met Theresa Dunlop. He had asked Roddy if he could go along to the dancing with him.

'What's got into you, Donald? I've been trying to drag you along to St Peter's for ages.'

St Peter's was a hall attached to a Catholic Church of the same name in Partick, where young people went dancing. It attracted both University students and young people from the west end and from Govan, which was only a short ferry journey over the Clyde.

'I've received a letter from Mary telling me when she's coming to Glasgow to begin her nursing studies and I know from her letters that she likes to dance. So, I thought if I could learn before she comes, then it would be something we could do together.'

The thought of Mary living in Glasgow excited him. He hadn't seen her since they had both left North Uist back in 1923, but they had corresponded faithfully during the intervening years. He wondered what she looked like now. She had been just a little girl the last time he saw her. Although he and Roddy had grown close again since he had come up to University, Mary was and would always be his closest friend.

'I don't know why she's coming up here. Surely there are plenty of places in Manchester where she could train to be a nurse.'

'I'm sure there are Roddy, but Mary thought it would be nice for us to meet up again after all these years. We have written faithfully to one another since we left North Uist, you know.'

'I know, but I can't understand why you wanted to keep in touch with her after what her mother did to our family. You're too soft Donald.'

Donald didn't reply. This was no place to have an argument with his brother, so he turned to look around him. This was his first time in a dance hall and although it was only a church hall and not as big and fancy as some places Roddy talked about, it was obviously very popular. There was a full orchestra tuning up, and the hall was absolutely packed with young men and women of similar age to them. There was an air of excitement as the men stood, casually smoking their cigarettes, eyeing up the girls who were waiting to be asked to dance. He broke into a sweat. What was he doing here?

As soon as the music began, Roddy was on the floor. He had to admit his brother cut a fine figure. Several girls watched him as he waltzed around the floor or jitterbugged with one pretty girl after another. He decided he better ask a girl to dance. Wasn't that the reason he had come here after all? But what a mistake that was.

The girl told him it was the Lindy Hop and tried to show him the steps, but he couldn't co-ordinate with her, so she left him high and dry on the floor. He then plucked up courage to ask another girl when a waltz came on, but he ended up standing on the girl's toes and she too walked off the floor. He should have joined a class to learn how to dance before coming here. What a fool he was.

In need of a drink, Roddy took a break from dancing and came to join him.

'So, are you enjoying yourself, Donald? Are you glad you came?'

'Yes, thanks, Roddy. But I'll need to take up dancing lessons if I'm to bring Mary to a place like this. I wouldn't want to hurt her by standing on her toes.'

Before Roddy could reply, they both noticed a couple dancing near them who were receiving a lot of attention from the crowd. People were nudging each other and pointing toward them. The girl was tall and slim with long black hair, and she looked slightly embarrassed as she danced around the room with a short, thin man, much shorter than herself. Roddy asked the young man who was standing next to him why people were watching them, and he told him the man was Benny Lynch, an up-and-coming boxer. Donald had never heard of him, not being a fan of fighting in any form. But he was to remember him a couple of years later when the newspapers reported he had won the British, European and World flyweight titles in Manchester.

As the girl made her way from the dance floor after she had finished dancing with the man, she moved towards them. Donald noticed how intently Roddy was looking at her and, obviously bewitched, he asked her to dance. There was a bit of flirting between them before she went back to join her friends. On the way home, all Roddy could talk about was his disappointment that the girl hadn't danced with him. He didn't think too much about it, but that girl was to become a huge part of Roddy's life over the next year and was to bring trouble to his door.

CHAPTER SEVENTEEN

Roddy was captivated as he watched Benny Lynch dance with the girl, their movements graceful and sensuous. Her coal black hair swung just above her shoulders, her hips swayed in time with the movement, and there was a twinkle shining flirtatiously from her eyes. He wondered if they were green or brown. He couldn't see from where he was standing. When the dance was over, she thanked her partner and moved across the floor toward Roddy. He thought she looked so elegant. Her fitted green dress swung in tune with her hips as she moved across the wooden floor in her high heels. As she came nearer, their eyes met, and he felt a tingle of anticipation that he hadn't felt in a long time. A faint blush bloomed on her cheeks, and he realised he must be looking at her too intensely as she lowered her eyes to the floor.

'Hello,' he said, 'I've been watching you dance.'

'Have you now?' she replied, raising her eyebrows in a perfect arch above her sea-green eyes as she looked into his.

'And I wondered if you would do me the honour of dancing with me.'

'Well, I might, but I would need to know who's asking me.'

'Of course, I'm sorry. My name's Roddy Macdonald. I'm a student at Glasgow University.'

'You don't sound like you come from Glasgow. Your voice is softer than the Glasgow boys I know; like Benny I was just dancing with.'

'You don't sound like you come from Glasgow, either. Are you Irish?'

'My Ma and Da are, but I was born and raised here. Probably their accents have rubbed off on me.'

'So, would you like to dance with me?'

'I need to powder my nose first, but I'll come and find you.'

'What's your name, if you don't mind me asking?' Roddy felt unusually shy about asking her, as she turned away from him.

'I'm Theresa Dunlop.'

'I'm pleased to meet you, Theresa Dunlop,' he said, holding his hand out towards her. She didn't take it, just turned on her heel and hurried over to her friends. When she got there, they all turned to look at him and giggled, then made their way to the powder room. He didn't see her again that night and assumed she must have gone home early. Donald told him his ears were sore, listening to him lamenting the fact that she hadn't come back.

He thought about her every night after that and couldn't wait for the next Friday to see if she would be there again. As he lay in bed at night, he was filled with desire as he imagined embracing her slender waist and drawing her close. He could almost feel her body pressing against his and the sweet smell from her mouth as she breathed lightly against his ear. By the time Friday came, he could think of nothing else.

'What's wrong with you Macdonald?' said Professor Harley. 'You look a million miles away.'

'Sorry Sir, just thinking about what I'll be doing this weekend.'

'Got a girl in mind, have you?'

'Maybe.'

'Well, don't forget the next heat in the debating competition is on Saturday, so keep a clear head for that. You might win the trip to Canada.'

Roddy had forgotten. He was so busy thinking about Theresa. He had entered the competition as he could win a trip to Canada to do a lecture tour of Canadian Universities if he won. And even if he didn't win, it would do his future career either as a politician or a solicitor no harm either. They went back to discussing the conveyancing laws of Scotland and then he was free.

He rushed home to his digs, ate the dinner Annie provided, then got ready for the evening. Neither Donald nor any of his friends were going dancing at St Peter's that night. One night was enough for Donald and his friends had other fish to fry. So he was going on his own. That didn't bother him. He wasn't shy and could talk to anyone. When he got there, the place was busy, and he scanned the room quickly to see if Theresa was there. She wasn't, and disappointment swept over him. He hung about with the other men at the side of the dance floor as if he were eyeing up the girls, although he had no interest in anyone else. Only in Theresa. He had almost given up hope when he spotted her. She was with the same friends as last week and was talking and laughing animatedly with them. She had her dark hair tied back with a red ribbon that matched the red lipstick she wore on her beautiful lips. Her teeth shone brightly when she laughed, and it surprised him to find his pulse racing. This was the first time he had felt this way. He watched as many young men asked her to dance and then decided it was his turn. He walked over to where she was standing, alone now as her friends had gone off somewhere.

'Hello again, Theresa,' he said. 'Do you remember me? Roddy. I wondered if you would like to dance.'

He put his hand on her arm and it felt like an electrode had given him a shock. He could see she felt it too by the way she jumped back from him.

'Sorry, I didn't mean to startle you.'

She smiled her special smile at him.

'I'd love to dance, thank you.'

She stepped closer to him. He placed his right hand on the small of her back and took her right hand in his, pulling her gently towards him. She seemed to tense and then her body relaxed, and they took to the floor. It was a slow waltz, and they didn't speak a word as they circled the floor in graceful movement, totally aligned. When the dance finished, he didn't need to ask her to dance again. It was unspoken that she was his partner for that night. They lost all track of time until one of her friends called to her that it was time to go.

'Come on, Theresa. Your Da won't be happy if you're late getting back.'

She gave a shrug, then leaned into him and whispered.

'My Da's an auld b******, so I don't like to get on the wrong side of him. Will I see you here next week? I've really enjoyed tonight.'

'Can't I see you before that, Theresa?'

'I'll see what I can do.' She smiled that wicked smile of hers, and his legs trembled as she placed a light kiss on his cheek. 'Where can I meet you?'

'I could meet you in Kelvingrove Park on Sunday if you like. I go to church in the morning, but I would be free in the afternoon.'

'Can you come over to Govan? It would be easier for me to meet you at the Pierce Institute on Govan Road after I've been to mass at St Anthony's.'

'Yes, okay. Shall we say twelve noon?'

And that was that. The beginning of the first love of his life. He was so besotted with her, he withdrew from the debating competition. The thought of going to Canada and being away from her for any length of time was unthinkable.

CHAPTER EIGHTEEN

Donald was excited. Mary was arriving in Glasgow today. They had arranged that he would meet her from the train and help her with her bags. He had asked Roddy if he wanted to go with him, but he had been less than enthusiastic.

'Why would I want to do that? I can't stand the girl.'

'How do you know? She's eighteen now and I dare say looks completely different from when she was a little girl back in 1923.'

He thought back to that year and the little girl with pigtails. She was a skinny wee thing, and he remembered how grateful he had been when she told him she didn't care if he was a Red Indian. No wonder he had wanted to hold on to her friendship.

'She wasn't to blame for what happened, Roddy. You told me we couldn't be blamed for the sins of our fathers, so she can't be blamed for the sins of her mother.'

'I know you're right Donald, but I'm sorry. I really don't want to see her. She was always your friend anyway, not mine, and besides, I've got a date with Theresa.'

He sounded like the angry young boy he used to be, jealous of Donald's friendship with Mary, as well as everything else. But then he relaxed and smiled.

'I'm sorry Donald. Tell her I said hello and perhaps we could all go dancing one night when she gets settled in.'

Despite taking private dancing lessons, he was no better a dancer now than he had ever been. He guessed it just wasn't his thing. He would need to think of other things to do with Mary and leave the dancing to Roddy.

'I'll tell her. Enjoy your date with Theresa. How are things going, by the way?'

'They're going well. She's the most beautiful girl I've ever met. The only problem is her father is pressing her to bring me home to meet him.'

'And why don't you want to go?'

'Well, although I love Theresa, going to meet her father will make our relationship a bit more serious, don't you think?'

'And you're not ready for that?'

'Not yet, although I can't wait for us to be together. You know. Go all the way. But I think that'll only ever happen when we marry. She says she's not that kind of girl.'

Donald felt a bit out of his depth. He had never had a girlfriend, let alone gone all the way, and wasn't sure what it would involve. He had guessed Roddy wanted to kiss and cuddle Theresa when he had asked him to make himself scarce, but clearly that wasn't going all the way. Donald had never been in love, but he had always thought that if he ever did meet someone, he would want to marry them.

'I think if you want to go all the way with Theresa, then you should meet her father and at least talk about marriage. It's not fair to string a girl along and ask her to go all the way if you have no intention of marrying her.'

Roddy laughed.

'Since when did you become such a man of the world?'

Donald blushed and bit the nail on his little finger. He hated when Roddy made fun of him.

'I'm only pulling your leg, Donald. You're right. I need to meet Theresa's father, so I'll tell her when I see her today. That's me off then. See you later.'

'Cheerio, Roddy. See you later.'

CHAPTER NINETEEN

It was a dismal rainy day when Mary arrived in Glasgow. She had to wipe away the condensation that had settled on the windows to see the city she was arriving in. From what she could see, it wasn't much different from Manchester. Another city that had made its fortune from the industrial revolution. But the weather didn't dampen her excitement at the thought of seeing Donald again. He was the reason she had chosen Glasgow to do her training. Now at Glasgow University and living with Roddy, she wondered if he was happier. She knew the Wall Street Crash had affected his financial situation and thanked her lucky stars her family had not been affected. The investments her grandfather had made seemed to have held their value. Glasgow Western Infirmary was close to Glasgow University, so it meant she could meet up with Donald on her days off. As it turned out, there were very few days off for her and the other trainees, so she didn't see as much of Donald as she thought she would.

When the train pulled in and stopped, she rose from her seat, reached her arms above her head, and yawned. It had been a long journey from Manchester, and she was stiff despite having walked up and down the corridor several times to stretch her legs. When she got off the train, she looked around expectantly, wondering if she would recognise Donald. It had been a long time since she had seen him and she was sure he must have changed, just as she had. There were several young men on the platform looking for passengers coming from the train, and she wondered if he was one of them. He was, but it wasn't until the others had met up with who they were waiting for that they each realised. They stood looking at one other for a moment before Donald came over to her.

'Hello, Mary?'

'Yes. I take it you're Donald. I didn't recognise you.'

'Nor me, you, but now that I know it's you, I can see the resemblance to that little girl I used to know. I'm sorry it's so miserable for your arrival. I have a taxi waiting for us.'

'It's not your fault, Donald. Thanks for ordering the taxi,' she said, impulsively placing a light kiss on his cheek.

He touched where her lips had been, and she could have sworn a blush crossed his cheeks. She thought he looked rather handsome. He had only been a boy the last time she saw him, but he had grown into a fine-looking man. Slightly taller than her, he had black hair which, although longer than the fashionable short back and sides men wore nowadays, was combed tidily into a side parting. As he looked down at her, she noticed his blue eyes were still the same piercing shade she remembered. She was conscious of an excited feeling in her tummy after she kissed him and wondered if he blushed because he was feeling the same as her. They had nothing to say to each other as they made their way out to Gordon Street to the taxi. But as soon as they got inside, they talked animatedly to one another, catching up on all they hadn't said in their letters.

When they got out from the taxi, Donald helped carry her luggage along to her accommodation at the Western Infirmary Training School. This is where she would spend the next three years. When she saw the building she would live in, it was a pleasant surprise. It looked like a house which had been extended and it turned out she was right. She found out later that the original house had belonged to someone called Donald James Macintosh, and she was to be one of the first nurses to do her training there. Eighteen single bedrooms were available for nurses in training with two for their sister tutors. There were also classrooms, a practice room, a sitting room, a library and two bathrooms for everyone to use.

She rang the bell, and it took a while for it to be answered. But eventually a woman, that Mary assumed was the housekeeper, opened it. When she saw Donald, she frowned.

'We do not allow gentlemen in the nurses' home. I'm afraid he will have to leave.'

'Oh, he's only helping me with my bags.'

'Well, he can place them here in the hallway and then be on his way.'

Donald dutifully put her suitcase in the hall and said his farewells.

'I shall contact you once I know when my days off are, Donald. It's been lovely catching up with you.'

She wanted to kiss his cheek again, but when she saw the woman looking at her, she decided against it. No point in getting into anyone's bad books before she had even begun.

When Donald had left, the woman introduced herself.

'I'm Mrs Munro, the housekeeper. Take a seat and I'll let Sister MacFarlane know you're here.'

Mary was nervous as she sat waiting for the Sister to arrive and while she was there, the doorbell rang again. Mrs Munro appeared from down the corridor, opened the door, and told the girl to come in and sit beside Mary. To Mary's surprise, she knew the girl. It was her friend from school, Cynthia Walters.

'Cynthia, what are you doing here?' she squealed with delight. 'I thought you were going into the Civil Service.'

'I changed my mind, Mary, and followed you to Glasgow. I was lucky. Someone dropped out, and I got their place.'

They hugged each other, delighted that they could carry on with their friendship in Glasgow.

'Better not let Sister MacFarlane see you hugging each other. She expects nurses to always act with decorum.'

When Mrs Munro had left, they looked at each other, giggled and hugged again. It would be such fun having Cynthia in her life again.

Before they could say any more, the Sister Tutor arrived.

'Good afternoon. I am Sister MacFarlane, one of two sister tutors who will teach you and your cohort while you are here. There will be a meeting for all the new arrivals at 7.30 pm in the sitting room. Make sure you are there on time. Punctuality is very important in nursing.'

The two girls nodded.

'Mrs Munro will show you to your rooms. You are very lucky. You will have a room for yourself. When I was training, I had to share with several other girls. Mrs Munro will serve a meal in the dining room at 5.30pm. Hopefully, all the girls will have turned up by then.'

Although the room was small, it had everything Mary needed. There was a bed and bedside cabinet, a chair, and a dressing table. She unpacked her clothes, put up a photograph of her mother and grandmother and her toiletries and hairbrush on the dressing table. She could hear noises out in the corridor, so opened the door and looked out. Mrs Munro was showing some other girls to their rooms. They looked like frightened rabbits. Mary was excited, rather than frightened. She couldn't wait to start her training and to take care of her patients. She didn't realise it would be some time before she would be let loose on members of the public.

1932

PREJUDICE AND INJUSTICE

CHAPTER TWENTY

Roddy and Theresa's relationship was a passionate one, with Theresa's desire for him matching his desire for her. But there were their families to consider, and all did not go well. When he wrote to tell his mother that he had met a lovely Catholic girl, she wrote back right away to say it was best not to get involved. *Catholics and Protestants don't mix, Roddy. It will only lead to heartache.* He ignored his mother. What did she know? She had led a very sheltered life and didn't know how different things were in a big city like Glasgow. At university, religion didn't seem to matter other than as part of theological debate. But he was wrong. It did matter, and it mattered to Theresa and even more so to her father.

After they had been going out for nearly a year, Theresa invited him to tea one Sunday afternoon to meet her family. The conditions they lived in shocked him. As well as Theresa, her mother, and father, there seemed to be several brothers and sisters. He wondered where they all slept, as there seemed to be only two rooms to accommodate them. Not that he was unused to overcrowded conditions. He knew lots of people on Uist had to share beds and bedrooms. But somehow the overcrowding on Uist didn't seem so bad as they all lived in single houses, rather than on top of one another the way people did in Glasgow tenements.

The house was clean and tidy, despite the number of people living in it, and her mother put on a grand tea for him with thick ham sandwiches and a Victoria sponge. Only he, Theresa, and her father and mother sat at the table to have the tea. He thought nothing of it until he noticed the younger children, who sat on the floor looking up at the table. He felt a tug of guilt when he saw them looking eagerly at the food, and knew they were waiting for leftovers, so decided against having any more sandwiches or cake.

Mr Dunlop had gripped Roddy's hand in greeting when he arrived.

'Hello, Roddy. I'm Patrick Dunlop, and I'm pleased to meet you... finally.'

Roddy wondered if he was being sarcastic. Also, he wasn't sure if he was supposed to call him Patrick or Mr Dunlop, so decided it was safer to be formal.

'I'm pleased to meet you too, Mr Dunlop. I'm sorry not to have met you sooner. I've been tied up with lots of studying and exams for the last few months.'

He nodded, but said nothing else. Thank goodness Mrs Dunlop was chatty as her husband just stared at him as he ate his sandwiches.

'So have you been to mass this morning, Roddy?' asked Mrs Dunlop

'Oh, yes. I've been to church. Going to church is a big thing on the island where I come from. We do very little else on a Sunday. I love living in Glasgow, as there don't seem to be so many restrictions.'

'So, you're not a Catholic?'

Roddy could sense the coolness in her voice and wondered why this was news. Hadn't Theresa told her parents he was a Protestant? He thought about what his mother had said in her letter. Maybe it was important after all.

'Church of Scotland, Mrs Dunlop.'

'I see. Well, you know our Theresa could never marry a Protestant. You would need to convert if you wanted to marry her.'

Marry her! He knew that's why her family had invited him over, but they were being rather direct. Didn't they realise he still had his course to finish, so he was in no position to marry anyone just now?

'I won't be able to get married until I finish my course, Mrs Dunlop. But perhaps you could explain what converting would involve.'

'Well, you would need to take instruction before you could marry in the Catholic church.'

'How long would that take?'

'Well, the church normally accepts new converts at Easter time.'

'I shall look into it, Mrs Dunlop. I love Theresa very much, but we haven't yet spoken of marriage, have we, Theresa?'

She blushed and said no; they hadn't, but perhaps they should.

He knew what she meant. It was growing harder and harder to stop themselves from making love. They did almost everything else, and it was wonderful, but oh, to enter her and take her totally would be so special. He could feel his arousal and decided he better stop thinking about her in that way and concentrate on the questions her mother and father were asking.

Her father then spoke up.

'Theresa tells me your landlord's a Communist. Are you a Communist?'

'I have a lot of sympathy for the Communists, Mr Dunlop, but I'm not a member of their party. I hope one day to become an MP.'

'An MP, you say. You're green behind the ears for that, young fellah, are you not?'

'I might be young, but I've got fire in my belly and a need to do something worthwhile with my life.'

Mr Dunlop looked sceptical.

'And what party would you stand as an MP for?'

Roddy felt annoyed. What business was it of his what party he supported? So he didn't give a direct answer.

'Well, I certainly wouldn't be supporting the Conservatives. They don't care about the workers.'

'And what would a student like you know about working men?'

'Now, now Patrick. We're not here to discuss Roddy's politics. We're here to talk about our daughter.'

He frowned at his wife's interruption, but when he next spoke, Roddy wished she hadn't stopped him from talking politics.

'Perhaps you and Theresa shouldn't see so much of each other, Roddy. I'm concerned you haven't thought yet about marrying my daughter even although you've been walking out with her for nearly a year. I don't want you ruining my girl's reputation. She shouldn't be running about so much with a man who hasn't even spoken to her about marriage.'

Roddy's heart sank, and he noticed tears in Theresa's eyes. The thought of not seeing her made him frantic, and a surge of anger towards her father made him speak unwisely.

'You're being unfair, Mr Dunlop. I love Theresa and have no intention of ruining her reputation. You can't stop us from seeing each other.'

He knew he had made a mistake when Mr Dunlop stood up, his face like thunder. Although they were a similar height, the man was a good few pounds heavier than him and his muscles made him look like a thin weakling. He wondered whether he could take him on if he punched him.

'My daughter will do as I tell her,' he bellowed. 'How dare you tell me what I can and cannot do where my daughter's concerned? You better leave this house now or you'll be sorry. And don't see my Theresa again until you've been to see a priest and I know your intentions towards her are decent.'

Roddy's heart was beating loudly in his chest, and he wanted to thump the man, but he couldn't do that in front of the women and children. They might get hurt, and that was the last thing he wanted.

'I'll go, Mr Dunlop. But don't think this is the end of things with Theresa. I love her and I will be with her.'

Theresa and Mrs Dunlop were now in tears, and Mrs Dunlop was holding onto her husband's arm, to stop him from pushing his fist into Roddy's face.

'Please go Roddy, you're only making things worse,' Theresa pleaded.

He was furious as he stomped out of the house, down the stairs and along the Govan Road to get the subway back over to Hillhead. He loved Theresa and wanted to be with her. How dare her father suggest he would spoil her reputation? What did he take him for? He was nothing but a bully and he was determined her father wouldn't stop him from seeing Theresa.

It was only later, when he had calmed down, that he reluctantly admitted that perhaps her father was right. If Theresa had let him, he would have gone all the way with her and wouldn't have thought a jot about her reputation. It was unfair of him to expect her to wait for him to finish his studies without at least giving her the security of an engagement to marry. He would find out more about becoming a convert and then see her father again to ask him for her hand. That would hopefully resolve her father's antagonism towards him. He must let his mother know what he planned to do.

CHAPTER TWENTY-ONE

I was livid when Roddy sent me a letter telling me he planned to become engaged to Theresa, the Catholic girl he had met at the dancing. I'd already told him Catholics and Protestants don't mix. What was he thinking? The thought of it is almost as bad as the thought of Donald marrying Mary Hepworth. Donald has now written to tell me Mary has moved to Glasgow to study nursing. How I wish she was going somewhere else to do it. Do they have no teaching hospitals in Manchester? I want nothing to do with the Hepworth family, for obvious reasons, but it turns out Donald and Mary have been writing to each other since they left North Uist in 1923. He had always relied too much on Mary's friendship when he was a boy, and I hoped things would change as he grew older and more independent. But according to Roddy, Donald is still awkward and shy with people, and he's delighted Mary is coming to Glasgow. There's little I can do about it, except hope that it doesn't turn into something more than friendship.

But what was I going to do about Roddy? I needed to get him to change his mind about marrying this girl. It would be a big mistake for them both. So, I sent him a telegram telling him that his father would turn in his grave if he married a Catholic. I knew it was unfair bringing his father into the discussion, but I had to make him see sense in any way I could. I also told him our family could not welcome a Catholic, so he would cut himself off from us if he married this girl. I wasn't being strictly honest when I said this, as I could never cut my son off, but it would be a difficult situation to live with. I hope my telegram will make him think again about what he's doing.

Thank goodness for my job. It stops me worrying all the time about my boys and the mistakes they might make. Heather has settled well into school, and I've settled well into my job back at the post office. Mr Simpson is a quiet man, who I think appreciates that I have the experience needed to just get on with the job I am paid to do. To avoid another incident like the one I experienced when he mentioned his wife had passed away, I stick to business and that seems to suit him too. The post office is busy with payments of pensions and the small subsidies the crofters receive from the government. Despite not having any stocks and shares, we have felt the impact of the Depression on the islands too. I hear from Shona McIver that keeping the shop going is hard, as people have less money to spend.

When I heard about the Crash of 1929, I was worried for Johnny, as he had mentioned investing in some stocks in the company he worked for. But it's been nearly three years, and he hasn't said much about how things are in Detroit now except that he still has a job to go to. He was thrilled with the photo of Heather I sent him. However, when he told me he hadn't shown the photograph to Janet as he thought Heather looked too much like him, I was worried. I hoped it didn't mean he and Janet were having problems again. Carrying this secret is a constant worry, and I hope it won't all blow up in my face one day.

CHAPTER TWENTY-TWO

He couldn't believe that religion could cause so much heartache. They were all Christians worshipping the same God. Why did it matter so much how people went about it? But then he remembered there had been schisms in the Presbyterian Church for that very reason. After he wrote to his mother telling her he hoped to become engaged to Theresa, she sent a telegram. *Your father would turn in his grave. We are Presbyterians Roddy, not papists. You must not do this. It will cut you off from your family if you do.*

Initially, her response annoyed him; she was trying to make him feel guilty by bringing his father into it and telling him his family would cut him off. What was so wrong about becoming a Catholic? He couldn't understand what all the fuss was about. Then he remembered how his father had reacted when Bunty Hepworth had organised a Christmas play. He had not been happy and had said that Christmas celebrations went against their Presbyterian way of life. He wanted to make his father proud, and marrying a Catholic would not do that, so he reluctantly had to admit that his mother was right. It was unthinkable to disappoint his father.

He spoke with Professor Nicholson to ask for his advice, as he was worried about his studies. Some of his professors had already told him he seemed to lack concentration. Professor Nicholson looked grave when he told him what the problem was.

'Well Roddy, this is a hard question you've come to me with and I'm not sure how to advise you. It depends how much you love this girl. Do you love her, or is it just lust or infatuation? It's important that you know which it is, as whatever decision you reach will have a profound effect on your life.'

'What do you mean, Sir?'

'You and this girl could end up being disowned by your families. From what you say, her father would never allow her to marry you without you becoming a Catholic, and if she did, then there is no doubt her family would disown her.'

He let Roddy think about this and then continued.

61

'And what about your family? They're Church of Scotland, I take it, so they won't be happy if you marry a Catholic. You could end up being estranged from them, too. Is this girl really worth that?'

Roddy thought back to what his mother had said and shuddered at the thought of what his father would have said on the subject. Perhaps it was just as well his father wasn't here to tell him. But he knew how he felt and couldn't envisage a time when he wouldn't want to have his mother, sister, and grandparents in his life. The Professor continued with additional reasons against marrying Theresa.

'There are also religious politics involved in this and it depends on what you want to do with your life. I know you're ambitious and harbour hopes of making a career in politics once you get your law degree. But marrying a girl on the wrong side of the fence, so to speak, and converting to Catholicism could put paid to that.'

When the professor said this, Roddy realised his friends had been acting differently towards him ever since he had started seeing Theresa. It seemed there was always some excuse not to socialise with him and Theresa when he asked them to go out.

'I take it there's no question of her joining the Church of Scotland?'

'No Sir. We've discussed it, and although she fears what her father would do to us, she fears more for her mortal soul. If she left, the church would excommunicate her, and she couldn't live with that. I just couldn't ask her to make that sacrifice.'

'Then I think you know what you must do, Roddy.'

CHAPTER TWENTY-THREE

There was a hunger march planned for September, so it didn't surprise Roddy when Jimmy asked him and Donald if they wanted to go along. What did surprise him was that Donald was interested. He had noticed that Donald was joining in their conversations and taking an interest in politics much more than he did when he first arrived in Glasgow. He didn't have as much to say as they did, but he was obviously taking in everything they were saying. Perhaps reading the Daily Worker and Communist pamphlets Jimmy had given him was having an effect.

'I hadn't planned to, Jimmy. I don't know about you Donald.'

'When is it? My new term will start in October.'

'It's on the 26th of September, so you could just make it. It's an important meeting for all working people, Donald. We'll be presenting our petition to the government, asking them to abolish the Means Test. It's a wicked assault on the working classes when unemployment is at one of its highest levels. I didn't fight and lose my leg in the war for this.'

Jimmy's face had grown red and there were tears of rage in his eyes. Roddy sympathised with him. So many young men had lost their lives, their limbs or their sanity in that bloody war, and there was nothing to show for it.

'You won't be able to go with your leg injury, will you?'

'I won't be able to march, no, but some of us are helping set up accommodation and kitchens for the marchers and we shall go either by bus or by car.'

'I would love to be there and see Ramsay MacDonald's face when we hand over the petition.'

'But we won't have time, Jimmy. How long will it take to march to London? We can't miss the start of the new term, Roddy,' Donald interjected.

'We reckon it will take less than a month and you could then go back by train. Just imagine seeing the Prime Minister's face when we hand over the petition.'

Roddy felt a quiver of excitement in his belly. Maybe he would get the chance to meet the man himself. A petition containing a million signatures demanding the abolition of the Means Test was to be handed to him. He envisaged himself and Jimmy striding up to Ramsay MacDonald and handing over the petition with a raucous crowd of marchers cheering them on. Although many Labour Party members saw Ramsay MacDonald as a traitor, Roddy wasn't one of them. He thought he had done the right thing in supporting the national government. It was the only way to stabilise the country in his opinion. He was confident Ramsay MacDonald would welcome the marchers and make sure their petition was handed over to parliament.

'Alright Jimmy, I'll help you out. Just let me know what I need to do. But I really must be back for my course starting in October. What about you, Donald? Will you join us?'

'I'm worried that we won't get back on time and besides, I've arranged to see Mary. But if you need help with anything before you go, Jimmy, I'll do what I can.'

Jimmy nodded his thanks and then turned to Roddy.

'Don't worry, Roddy. I'll make sure you get back on time.'

But Jimmy was in no fit state to make sure he was back in time for his course. The march had been everything and nothing like he thought it would be. He had felt so proud when he set out with the columns of marching men with their knapsacks and blankets on their backs. There was an air of excitement as they all marched on their way to London to fight for the abolition of the hated Means Test. Bands played, flags flew, and the men were cheery and determined. He, Jimmy, and even Donald had done some fundraising beforehand. They had been grateful for the donations of the cooperative and the trade unions, but the way the government had treated those men was a disgrace. He and others who were trying to get accommodation for the marchers had to fight tooth and nail to get it. In the end, it was mostly ordinary people like themselves who had helped them.

64

The government sent agents to mix with the marchers to stir them up and find out who the ringleaders were. To his shame, one of them had fooled him and everyone else. He was a man in his mid-thirties and seemed so genuine. He told them he came from Manchester and had lost his job in the mill he worked in when it closed because of the recession. His child had died of malnutrition and lack of medical care when she became ill. Everyone felt sorry for him and didn't realise that all he was doing was gathering information to pass on to the police. He had seen the man in Hyde Park later that day, pointing out Jimmy to the mounted police.

He would never forget the terror he felt when they charged the marchers. Everyone scattered, but there were lots of casualties as the police weighed into them with their truncheons. Jimmy was one of seventy-five casualties of the police assault, and he ended up in hospital. How could a Labour government allow such a thing to happen? And that traitor Ramsay MacDonald didn't even have the courtesy to accept the Marcher's petition. The march changed him forever. He thought his career might be in politics, but it was a filthy business and he wanted nothing to do with it.

CHAPTER TWENTY-FOUR

Donald had hardly seen Mary since he had dropped her off at her accommodation. So, when he received her note telling him she had an afternoon off and would love to see him, he was delighted. Although it meant he couldn't go on the hunger march with Jimmy and Roddy, it was worth it just to meet her. Touching his cheek, he remembered the kiss she had given him when he met her from the train. He had a reaction he hadn't felt since his teenage years when puberty had struck. He couldn't wait to see her again and hoped everything was going well for her. The housekeeper at the nurses' home was a bit of a dragon and had made it clear he would not be welcome there. So he couldn't even go around on the off chance that he might meet her.

She had a lot to tell him as they settled into The University Café on Byres Road.

'Nursing is not quite what I was expecting, Donald. I've hardly seen a patient. We've spent most of our time in the classroom. And when we've had the odd day on the ward, the Sister and the Staff Nurses treated us like skivvies rather than nurses. They constantly boss us about, telling us to clean down the walls and floors.'

'That's rotten for you. Can't you complain?'

'No. Trainee nurses are the lowest of the low and we need to do what we're told or we'll get a black mark against us. But enough about me. What about you?'

'I'm fine and enjoying university life much better than I enjoyed school.'

'Why is that Donald?'

'Partly because of Roddy as he includes me in lots of things. But I've also joined a Writer's Group and am on the editorial board of the Gilmorehill Globe. I'm enjoying it all immensely.'

As he said the words, he realised he was enjoying life and having Mary here was the icing on the cake. He decided not to tell her he had also joined the Young Socialists, as he wasn't sure what her politics were, and he didn't want to put her off.

'What do you write?'

'For the newspaper, I just write the occasional article about what's happening at the university, but in terms of my creative work, nothing much yet. Just short stories and poems, but I hope to write a novel one day.'

'You must let me read what you've written so far.'

'Oh, they're not good enough to let anyone read, I'm afraid.'

'I'm sure you're being too modest, Donald. But I won't force you to show me them if you don't want to. And Roddy, how is he?'

'He's okay. He had a girlfriend, a Catholic girl, but things haven't worked out as he hoped, so he's naturally upset. But he's taken his mind off it by going on the Hunger March to London. He's hoping he'll see Ramsay MacDonald when they present the petition against the Means Test. He and Jimmy, our landlord, invited me to go too, but I wanted to see you.'

She blushed and blinked her eyes several times, but said nothing.

'How is your mother?' he asked, for something to say.

'I don't really know. She only writes occasionally now, and her letters are always positive, so I assume all is going well with her. I think I told you she stayed in Canada when she went to visit where her father lived. She's a schoolteacher in Saltcoats now, which is the nearest town to where Auntie Chrissie and Uncle Roderick lived and where you were born.'

For some reason he didn't understand, Donald found himself with a lump in his throat when he thought about his birth and about Chrissie and Roderick. He had thought they were his parents, and they had treated him like their son. He sometimes missed them so much. Mary sensed his sadness and put her hand on his. He felt himself shiver at her touch and responded by putting his hand over hers.

'I think I would like to go to Canada one day to see where I was born and to find out more about my mother. Although I tell no one about her or that I have Indian blood. I'm scared they'll make fun of me the way the children did at school. Do you remember?'

'I remember Donald. I kind of understand how you feel as I tell no one about my mother's mental health problems. I feel so ashamed of what she did and have to confess sometimes I'm scared something like that could happen to me.'

Donald's heart melted when she told him this. It made him want to hold her close and comfort her, but he was too shy to follow his feelings. She might think him too forward and put a stop to their friendship. He couldn't bear it if she did, but her next words gave him such hope for their continuing relationship.

'Perhaps we could go to Canada together when we finish our studies. I could visit my mother and you could visit the homestead you were born on and see your mother's grave. It would be good to have an adventure before we begin our working lives.'

'That sounds a grand idea, Mary.' He paused, then said, 'I love having you here, you know. I've never had a friend like you.'

She blushed and blinked her eyes again, and he wondered if he had said too much.

'Look, I'm going to have to get back to the training unit or the Sister will have my guts for garters, although I could spend the whole day with you. I've so enjoyed our conversation.'

Donald's heart missed a beat. She felt the same as him and wished they could spend more time together. He beamed a smile at her and grabbed her hand, pulling her up from her seat.

'Right, well, let's get going then. I can't have you getting into trouble on my account. That Sister might never let you out of the nurses' unit again, and I won't ever get to see you.'

Mary had told him that even though the rules allowed trainees to have one day off a month and a half day once a week, they rarely got their full complement of leave. The Sister was all-powerful and could make a decision that the ward was too busy to spare them, so it was important to keep on the right side of her. They left the café hand in hand before realising what they were doing and quickly pulled apart. But Donald felt he was walking on air all the way home.

CHAPTER TWENTY-FIVE

Donald missed Roddy while he was away on the March and wished he could have met Mary another time, so that he could have gone with him. But Mary was more important. So, as a compromise, he had agreed to help Jimmy and Roddy with fundraising. The marchers would need food and accommodation, and that didn't come for free. He had more than enjoyed his day with Mary and wouldn't have missed it for the world. But he read the reports every day in the Daily Worker of what was happening with the marchers so that he could chat with Jimmy and Roddy about it when they got back. When Roddy didn't return in time for the start of the new term, Donald knew something had gone wrong. His plan had been to leave London by train as soon as they had handed over the petition, but he hadn't turned up in Glasgow when expected.

He and Annie waited in suspense to find out what had happened. Before long, Annie received a message from Harry McShane of the National Unemployed Workers Movement explaining all that had gone on. She cried when she read of the awful things that had happened in London and that Jimmy was in hospital. He was a casualty of the mounted police assault on the marchers in Hyde Park and would come home by bus once he was well enough.

'The comrades have arranged that for him and the others who were injured in their fight for justice,' said Annie, wiping her eyes.

Although he was no longer sure there was a God, he prayed Jimmy would be okay,

When Roddy arrived back home with Jimmy, he was a changed man. He hated the national government and what they had done, especially Ramsay MacDonald.

'What a bloody traitor he is, Donald. I shall never vote for Labour again and I will never go into politics. It's a filthy business and I want none of it.'

He became quite morose. What with splitting up with Theresa and his disillusionment with his hero, he seemed to have lost his spark. So, to cheer him up, he invited Roddy to take him and Mary to the dancing,

'Theresa could be there, so you would have the chance to let her know what you've decided.'

'Okay Donald. Only because I need to see Theresa, not because I want anything to do with Mary Hepworth.'

CHAPTER TWENTY-SIX

The last thing Roddy wanted to do was to go dancing or to meet Mary Hepworth. But when Donald invited him to take her dancing, he agreed only because he hoped he might meet Theresa there. He hadn't been able to talk to her yet to tell her his decision. He was sure she must be wondering what he had decided.

'Mary's getting a pass to come out today, Roddy, so I thought it would be nice to take her for ice cream to the University Café. Then maybe you could take her dancing to that St Peter's dance hall you're so fond of. You haven't seen her for years and when you meet her again, you'll see she's turned into a very attractive young woman.'

'Has she now? And does my wee brother have a crush on her?'

'Don't be daft, Roddy. Mary and I are just friends.'

'Aye, that's what we all say when we start out. We'll see what happens.

'Anyway, are you happy to come for ice cream and then take her dancing? It's on this afternoon, isn't it?'

'Yes, it is. But won't you mind not getting to spend time with her?'

Roddy smiled as Donald's face fell.

'I hadn't thought of that. I just wanted to do something that would make Mary happy. Perhaps I should come dancing too. It might please her that I'm attempting to do something she enjoys.'

I'm sure it will. But I'm only going along to please you; not to please that witch Bunty's daughter. How is she getting on, by the way? Has she recovered and got out of the asylum?'

'Of course she has. She was only in it for a year. Poor woman. I hear it's terrible the way they treat people in these asylums. The so-called psychiatrists give the patients electric shock treatment, and some even get their brains operated on.'

Roddy shuddered at the thought.

'Mrs Hepworth lives in Canada now. She left Manchester when Mary was 12 and now lives in Saltcoats. That's the town near to where we lived with your mother and father in Canada.'

'What's she doing there?'

'She's working as a teacher. Apparently, she wanted to see where her father lived before he died, and she also wanted to find Uncle Johnny.'

'Uncle Johnny? Why would she want to find him?'

'I'm not sure, but that's what Mary told me.'

As far as he was concerned, the whole family was twisted, and he wished Mary had done her nurses' training elsewhere. He knew his mother agreed. She was worried that the friendship between Donald and Mary might develop into something else, and she could think of nothing worse.

CHAPTER TWENTY-SEVEN

Mary and Donald continued to meet whenever she got some time off, although she also went out with Cynthia and some of the other trainees when she got the chance. They liked to go to the pictures or to the dancing, as it was a welcome distraction from the hard work and sometimes heartache involved in being a nurse. She and the other trainees had now been let loose on the public and she at last felt she was doing what she came to Glasgow to do. Although they seemed to spend most of their time in the sluice emptying and cleaning bedpans, they also got the chance to work directly with the patients. She was in the men's medical ward and had learned a lot about the male body, which looked somewhat different from what the textbooks showed.

Cynthia had met several boys at the dancing, and she now had a steady boyfriend who worked in the City Chambers as a clerk for the local council. His job was to attend council meetings and take notes. He even got to meet the Lord Provost sometimes. It impressed Cynthia that her boyfriend was mixing with people in such elite circles. Although she had been on several dates with different men she had met at the dancing, Mary had met no one yet that she liked enough to consider having him as a boyfriend. Donald sometimes took her to the pictures, but he would not go dancing. He said he was left-footed and wouldn't be able to do it. His preference was taking her for a walk in the Botanic Gardens to visit the Kibble Palace or visiting the Glasgow Art Gallery on Argyle Street. Sometimes they would even catch a bus to Hogganfield Loch and have a picnic of boiled egg sandwiches and lukewarm tea from a flask that he brought along. She loved these times, and Cynthia said she thought she was in love with Donald. She hotly denied it, saying they were just friends, but sometimes she wondered if she was. He was so easy to be with; it felt like she was part of him and he of her. Perhaps it was because they were second cousins or whatever their relationship was.

So, on this day, she had a spring in her step and happiness in her heart as she made her way to meet Donald at the University

Café on Byres Road. He said he had a surprise for her, and she wondered what it was. If she had known, she wouldn't have gone. It was a fine Autumn day, and the trees were dressed in beautiful brown, russet, ochre, and yellow leaves. The odd one occasionally floated down from above and made Mary blink as it floated past her. She felt free. It was sometimes like being in a nunnery in the nurses' home and wished she could skip down the road rather than walk sedately as a young woman of her station should.

She stood outside the café for a few minutes, but when it began to drizzle, she went and sat inside. Not long after she sat down, she heard the door opening and turned to see Donald standing, looking around for her in his shy and uncertain way. Her heart melted, and she called his name. His face lit up when he saw her, and he hurried over to the booth she was sitting in. But he wasn't alone. He had a man with him who stood tall and sure of himself, and Mary wondered who it could be.

'Sorry to have kept you waiting.'

'Hello Donald,' she said, holding out her hand, which he took and shook enthusiastically. 'I was early.'

'This is Roddy. You remember him, don't you, Mary? As you know, he and I share lodgings. This is the surprise I was telling you about. I've asked him to take us dancing, as I know how much you like it.'

'Yes, of course I remember Roddy,' she said, holding out her hand in greeting.

He hesitated for just a second before taking her hand, then replied.

'Hello Mary. It's nice to see you again.'

She was aware of a spark of hostility coming from him and cursed herself when her eyelids began fluttering involuntarily. Blinking like this was something she hated. It was worse than blushing as it was a sure sign she was nervous, and she realised she didn't want him to think she was nervous.

'And you. How are you finding living in Glasgow after the remoteness of the Hebrides?'

74

'I love it. There are so many things to do here, and it's wonderful having the freedom to do exactly as I like without my mother spying on me. But what made you come to Glasgow? I'm sure there are teaching hospitals in Manchester.'

'Yes, you're right. But I chose Glasgow because Donald was here. I knew I should have a dear friend to help me if I grew lonely.'

She patted Donald's hand, as close to a hug as she could reasonably get away with, and then they both smiled affectionately at each other.

'Not that I shall have much time to be lonely. I live in accommodation with a lot of other girls just like me, and we must ask for a pass any time we want to go out. They treat us like nuns rather than nurses.'

She and Donald laughed, but Roddy just lifted the menu to see what type of ice cream to order. She wished he would be a little less hostile. The sound of the Italian owners chatting in their own language seemed loud as the three of them sat in silence, choosing what they would have.

CHAPTER TWENTY-EIGHT

Roddy and Donald left Jimmy's flat and made their way to the University Café to meet Mary. An Italian family ran the café and served traditional favourites, like spaghetti bolognese and delicious ice cream. When they got inside, Mary was there. Not that Roddy recognised her straight away. He had noticed the pretty girl with long honey-coloured hair sitting in a booth but hadn't been aware she was Mary. Not until Donald's face lit up when he saw the girl, and then he knew. From the soft way they looked at each other, they were more than friends, but it was clear they didn't know it.. He would need to think of something to put them off finding out. Perhaps taking her to the dancing would be a good idea, as she might meet some other bloke there who could take her off his brother's hands. Donald wasn't the most exciting of people, so it shouldn't be too hard to find someone from amongst his friends to distract her. Despite these thoughts, he felt slightly envious of Donald and Mary and wished his relationship with Theresa wasn't so complicated.

'This is Roddy. You remember him, don't you, Mary?'

'Yes, of course,' she smiled, and he noticed her teeth were white and even. This made him think of Theresa and how her teeth had shone so white against her red lipstick. Then he noticed she was blinking her eyes rather a lot and wondered if she had a nervous tick or if she was feeling awkward about meeting him. Probably the latter, as she had a lot to feel awkward about.

'Hello Mary,' he said coolly. 'It's so nice to see you again.'

She was a fool if she believed that, but then he noticed a blush bloom across her cheeks and regretted his incivility. He supposed it wasn't her fault that her mother was a bad yin. But it didn't stop him from later raising the question of her mother when there was a lull in the conversation.

'May I ask you how your mother is getting along? The last time I saw her was the day of my father's funeral. I believe she made a bit of a show of herself and ended up getting locked up.'

Mary's face went pale at his words and her eyes began blinking rapidly again. She looked over at Donald, probably expecting him to stand up for her, but she obviously didn't know Donald as well as she thought. Her eyes glistened with tears, and he felt a little ashamed that he had upset her. But she was a feisty wee thing, as she stood up for herself.

'My mother was ill, and that's why she did what she did, Roddy, as you well know.'

'I'm sorry if I've upset you, Mary. It wasn't my intention.'

But, of course, it was, and he could tell she knew it.

'Donald, if you don't mind. I think I'll just have some tea and then make my way home. We've been working flat out this week and I'm so tired, I just want to go home and flop into my bed.'

'But I've asked Roddy to take you dancing, Mary. I know how much you enjoy it. And I would come too.'

Poor Donald. He was doing his best to smooth things over, but it didn't work.

'That was a very kind thought, Donald,' she said, then turned to him.

Roddy, I hope you don't mind me not going dancing with you. I'm absolutely worn out.'

'Of course not, Mary. You must look after yourself. Perhaps we can make a date for another time.'

'Yes, that would be nice.'

He ate his ice cream with relish, feeling a little triumphant that he seemed to have won a minor victory over Mary. She and Donald sat there miserably, hardly touching their food. As soon as they finished; she and Donald went off to walk back to the Western while he went to the Men's Union. As he watched them leave, he rationalised his actions by convincing himself she deserved it. Her mother had hastened his father's death as far as he was concerned.

CHAPTER TWENTY-NINE

When they finished their ice cream, Donald walked Mary back to the nurses' home, while Roddy went along to the Men's Union. She was quiet on the short walk, only nodding or saying a 'yes' or 'no' to his nervous attempts at conversation. He felt sick. She was bound to stop their friendship after what had happened with Roddy. Why hadn't he said something, anything, to show he disapproved of Roddy's behaviour towards her? As they approached Church Street, Donald decided on a plan of action to cheer Mary up and hopefully win her round.

'Mary, I know Roddy upset you and I apologise. Why don't you and I go to a matinee in the Salon picture house? Grand Hotel with John Barrymore and Greta Garbo is showing. It's supposed to be good.'

When she didn't respond, he continued.

'I know how much you love your time off and I hate to think of you just lying in your tiny room feeling upset because of my lout of a brother.'

Mary's hesitation didn't surprise him. What Roddy had said about her mother was unforgivable, and yet he had said nothing to support her. He was ashamed of his cowardice and hoped she would find it in her heart to forgive him. He held his breath, waiting for her answer.

'You've nothing to apologise for, Donald, and I thank you for your offer. I would love to go to the Salon. I just couldn't bear to spend any more time with your brother. I'm sorry.'

'He can be overbearing, but he has a kind heart. He just keeps it well hidden sometimes.'

They smiled at one another and before he knew it, she was clasping his hand in hers and leading him away from the nurses' home. As they walked, she told him about her first month on the ward, which was in Men's Medical, where she was never out of the sluice, emptying bottles and bedpans. She blushed prettily when she told him that working in the men's ward was an eye-

78

opener, as she had never seen a man's private parts before. Donald found himself inordinately pleased when she told him that.

'But I've seen them aplenty this month. We must do what's called the back round in the morning and the evening for the men who are confined to bed.'

'The back round. What's that?'

'It means we nurses must wash and dry the men's delicate areas.'

She made a funny face and a gesture with her hands when she said this, which made Donald laugh. He wondered what it would be like to have Mary wash and dry his delicate parts, but he couldn't linger there, as she had lots more to tell him.

'But I've so enjoyed working with the patients and gradually got to know some of them well. So, you can imagine how upset I was when one patient died. It was so sad to think of him being alive one day and not the next. But the worst part was I had to help the staff nurse prepare the man to be taken to the mortuary by the hospital porters.'

Donald's stomach became queasy at the thought and hoped she wouldn't give him the intimate details of this part of her job.

'You must have a stronger constitution than me, Mary. I don't think I would have the stomach for it.'

'As it turned out, I didn't. I actually fainted, would you believe?'

'Oh no, that must have been terrible for you.'

'I was so embarrassed, but I suppose I'll get used to it. I'm only at the start of my training but I was worried that fainting on the job would get me a black mark and it did.'

'What happened?'

'Sister sent me to the Matron's office after giving me a cup of hot sweet tea to revive me.'

'Not medicinal brandy, then?'

'Ha, ha, as if. I probably wouldn't have drunk it though even if she had given me it. I rarely drink alcohol.'

'No, me neither. I had a beer and a whisky one night when I went out with Roddy, but it made me feel awful, so I decided I wouldn't have it again.'

'I think you're wise, Donald. My mother sometimes drank sherry in the evenings, and she became quite maudlin with it.'

Luckily, they had reached the Salon, so the discussion didn't go any further. But it was clear to Donald, from the way she had gone pale when Roddy mentioned her mother, that what had happened could still upset her.

CHAPTER THIRTY

Roddy decided he needed to see Theresa and tell her their relationship was over, although she probably guessed as much by now as he hadn't seen her for weeks. He wanted to be with her more than anything, but his life was just beginning. It was too much to ask him to give up his family and possibly his career and equally he couldn't ask her to give up her family and her religion, which meant so much to her. There was nothing else for it. They would need to separate and go their own ways. Having decided, he knew the honourable thing to do was to tell her. It would be wrong to just disappear from her life without an explanation. But how could he contact her? He thought about writing a letter, but what if her mother or father intercepted it and didn't give it to her? No, he would need to tell her face-to-face. It was the right thing to do. He talked to Donald about it and Donald agreed he should see Theresa.

'The only problem is, I can't go to the house, for obvious reasons, and I can't go to her work. I tried that and luckily spotted Mrs Dunlop standing outside before she spotted me. Her father has obviously put a watch on her to make sure I don't get in touch.'

'What about St Peter's? You were hoping you might see her that day when I asked you to take Mary dancing.'

'It's worth a try. But I can't see her father letting her go there on her own.'

'I'll come with you. If we go early and wait outside until she arrives, you can then talk to her in private while I keep a lookout for her father.'

'He's an absolute brute of a man, Donald. I hope he isn't waiting to see if I turn up. I mean, I'm doing what he wants after all.'

'Well, maybe he won't see it like that. Perhaps he would prefer you to convert and marry Theresa and if he's as hot-headed as you say he is, things could get nasty.'

Roddy hadn't thought of that. It seemed that no matter what he did, it would be wrong.

81

It was early evening when they made their way along to the dance hall. He felt as if his life was over rather than just beginning. He couldn't imagine life without Theresa, but he couldn't imagine life with her, either. It was impossible. He hated what he was about to tell her, but there was no other way for them. When he and Donald reached Hyndland Street, they scanned the entrance to see if there was any sign of Theresa or her father. They must have waited for half an hour before they, at last, saw Theresa. But she was with her father. Roddy ducked into the alley at the side of the hall so that they wouldn't see him, while Donald told him what was happening. Theresa's father wouldn't recognise Donald, as he had never met him.

'It looks like Theresa's father is going into the pub on the corner while she goes dancing. That's her away inside now and her father has gone into the pub. This is your chance, Roddy.'

They hurried along to the entrance, where they spotted Theresa putting her coat into the cloakroom. Roddy went over quickly and called her name.

'Theresa, keep your coat. I need to talk to you. Please come outside.'

She looked scared, and he understood why.

'My Da's just in that pub on the corner. What if he sees us?'

'He'll be too busy drinking his beer and my brother Donald will keep an eye out for him while we talk.'

He grabbed her hand and pulled her with him into the alley.

'What are you doing here, Roddy? My father will kill you if he finds out you've tried to see me.'

'He won't find out, Theresa. I'm not coming into the dancing, but I just had to speak to you one last time. I couldn't just never see you again.'

'Oh Roddy. I wish it didn't have to be like this,' she said, tears spilling from her eyes.

'Oh, my darling, so do I. Please don't cry. I can't bear to see you upset.'

He pulled her into his arms, and they kissed like they never had before. They both knew it was their last kiss and became quite carried away, forgetting that they were in a public place for anyone to see. As bad luck would have it, it was Father Lafferty, the local Parish priest who saw them. Donald hadn't noticed the danger as he was too busy looking for Theresa's father coming out of the pub.

'Theresa Dunlop, what the hell do you think you're doing behaving like a harlot outside the church hall? I'll be having a word with your father. Get away from that man.'

Roddy would never forget the look of terror in Theresa's eyes as she turned and saw the old priest.

'Oh, please don't tell my Da, Father Lafferty. This is the last time I'll ever see Roddy. I promise you.'

'It is the last time, Father Lafferty,' said Roddy. 'We know we can never be together because of the difference in our religion. We just had to say goodbye to each other one last time.'

The priest regarded him suspiciously and pursed his lips, ready to say something, but Roddy continued.

'Please don't tell Mr Dunlop. You don't know what he's like. Please let Theresa go to the dancing and let her father pick her up as they had planned. I won't ever see her again after this.'

The priest didn't have time to reply as Donald shouted that Mr Dunlop had left the pub and had spotted them. As Roddy turned to see where he was, he saw him standing under a gas streetlamp, smoking a cigarette. Before he could do anything, the man threw his cigarette to the pavement and ground it under his steel toe-capped boot.

CHAPTER THIRTY-ONE

Donald couldn't believe it when he saw Mr Dunlop race across the road. For a man of his age, he was quick, and Donald moved out of his way. The first thing the man did was grab Theresa by her hair and fling her to the ground. Luckily, he caught her before she fell. But when Mr Dunlop started to punch and kick into Roddy, he found himself immobile. Although the extent of the beating his brother was receiving alarmed him, he could do nothing. Before he could pull himself together, Patrick Dunlop had knocked Roddy out and was pulling his daughter by the arm. He heard someone shouting to call the police or a doctor and the next thing he was aware of was the sound of an ambulance. His legs were shaking as the men put Roddy on a stretcher and lifted him into the back of the ambulance. The sight of Roddy's blood-soaked clothing filled Donald with dread, and made him fear the worst.

'May I come with him, please? He's my brother.'

'Get in quick. He looks in a bad way and we'll need to get him to the Western as quickly as we can,' said a stretcher-bearer.

Donald jumped in and sat down on the bed opposite. The ambulance went at speed and shook Donald about the entire way to the Western all the while its bell ringing loudly to warn other vehicles of its approach. He felt sick with the motion, but more so with himself. He couldn't believe he had done nothing to help Roddy. Images of the man kicking his boot into him flashed before his eyes. How could he have been such a coward to let that man treat his brother like that? He hoped the police would arrest him and send him to jail.

When they arrived at the hospital, the ambulancemen rushed Roddy inside while Donald was told to wait in the reception area. He was called over and asked to give Roddy's details and then told to take a seat.

'Someone will come and see you once we have assessed him,' said the nurse on duty. Donald wondered if Mary was on duty tonight. He prayed she was, as it would do him the world of good if he could see her. He sat down on a hard chair and waited, it

84

seemed, for hours. The clock on the wall ticked loudly the whole time and at one point, he felt he wanted to throw something at it to make it stop. He was sitting with his head in his hands when he heard the nurse calling his name.

'Mr Donaldson!' She opened the glass hatch she was sitting behind. 'I've been told to let you know they have taken your brother up to the Men's Medical ward. The doctor tells me he appears not to have sustained any serious injuries, but they will keep him in for observation. You can go home now.'

'But can't I see him? I want to see for myself that he's okay.'

'I'm sorry. No visitors allowed.'

Donald didn't argue as the nurse closed the hatch again with a snap, signalling the matter was not up for discussion. He didn't know what to do and went outside onto Church Street. Mary's accommodation was just round the corner, and he found himself walking there. When he arrived at the front door, he rang the bell. A burly man in a uniform opened the door.

'What kind of time is this to come here? It's nearly ten o'clock. Clear off.'

'Please. I must see Mary Hepworth.'

'She'll be in her bed by now if she's anyway decent. If you don't move, I shall have to tell Sister and she'll be in trouble.'

The man banged the door in his face. He could have cried. He heard a movement behind him and saw a young woman staring at him, and it was obvious she had heard him speaking to the man.

'Hello. Are you Donald? Is it Mary you're looking for?'

'Yes. My brother's been injured and is in the hospital. I'm not allowed to see him and was hoping Mary could visit him for me tomorrow and then let me know how he is.'

'What's your brother's name and which ward is he in?'

Donald told her.

'I'll let her know,' the girl said, looking at him sympathetically. 'She'll do her best for you, I'm sure.'

'Thank you. You are very kind.'

The girl rang the bell, and the same burly man came to the door. 'What time do you call this Cynthia Walters? Get in before anyone sees you.'

He had a smile on his face until he saw Donald was still there.

'I told you to clear off. If you don't move, I'll call the police and you'll end up in the cells.'

'I'm going. Thank you again, Miss Walters,' he said, and with that, he turned and trudged home feeling an abject failure.

CHAPTER THIRTY-TWO

Mary was just getting ready for bed when she heard a knock at her door. She opened it and was surprised to see Cynthia standing with her outdoor clothes on. She was looking around her furtively, obviously worried that the Sister Tutor might discover her.

'Cynthia. Come in. What's wrong?'

'Nothing's wrong, Mary. I've had an enjoyable time at the pictures with Jack. He's so lovely, and he kissed me tonight. Just on the cheek, you understand, but still.'

She looked dreamy, and Mary wondered if she had just come to tell her about this kiss.

'That's wonderful for you, Cynthia, but I really need to get to bed. I'm on day shift tomorrow.'

'Oh yes, so am I. Sorry. I came to tell you that Donald, the boy you're soft on, was standing outside the front door when I came home.'

'Donald?'

'Yes. He wanted to give you a message, but Graeme sent him packing. I took pity on him and said I would tell you.'

'So, what was his message?'

Mary began blinking as she waited for Cynthia to tell her what Donald had said.

'He said his brother, Roddy, is in Men's Medical. He's not allowed in to see him and wonders if you could go to find out how he is.'

'Roddy? In the hospital? I wonder what's happened to him. Did Donald tell you?'

'No, he didn't, and I didn't think to ask. Sorry.'

'Thanks for letting me know, Cynthia. I'm on that ward just now, so I'll be able to check on him.'

When Cynthia had left to go to her own room, she went back to bed but couldn't sleep even though she was exhausted. Her mind scurried about, wondering what had happened to Roddy. She didn't like him, but she didn't like to think he was seriously ill, as it would upset Donald.

The next morning, she slept in and got a telling-off from Sister Crawford when she arrived five minutes late. They were in the middle of doing the ward handover report, so she listened intently to hear what they said about Roddy.

'We have a new patient on the ward today. His name is Roddy Macdonald,' said the Sister reading her notes. 'He received a terrible beating and was brought in by ambulance last night. He has a concussion, is badly contused, and has cracked ribs.'

It shocked Mary when she saw Roddy. He was almost unrecognisable. His usually good-looking face was grotesquely swollen and had purple and blue bruises all over. His eyes were thin slits in his puffed-up cheeks and his lips were misshapen. The only parts of his body she could see were his face and neck, but the state they were in told her the rest of his body would be the same. He was asleep or unconscious and looked vulnerable lying in the hospital bed. The doctor must have sedated him to ease his pain.

'What on earth happened to him?' she asked the nurse on duty.

'I'm not sure, but the police came in to question him last night, poor man, but he was in no fit state to talk to them.'

'Is he going to be okay? I need to let his brother know how he is.'

'The doctor thinks he will be all right, although it was a vicious attack by the looks of it.'

'How long will they keep him in?'

'Probably about a week. But I think he'll need lots of bed rest when he gets home.'

Mary moved over and took Roddy's hand, but there was no response.

Just then, a loud voice called her name. It was Sister Crawford.

'Mary Hepworth,' she bawled. 'What do you think you're doing? I'm told you're a friend of this young man. Well, our rules do not permit nurses to visit their boyfriends whenever it suits them.'

'He's not my boyfriend, Sister. He's my friend's brother and as he can't visit him, he asked if I would find out how he was.'

'I see. Okay then, but get on with your work now.'

As she went about her duties, she couldn't get the image of Roddy out of her mind. He must have got a terrible beating and Donald must have been with him. She thanked God that whoever had done this terrible thing to Roddy hadn't hurt Donald. Her heart pounded when she thought of Donald being injured like that.

When Sister Crawford went for her lunch, Mary went over to Roddy's bed. Sister had made sure she would not be involved with Roddy's care, for which she was grateful. Doing the back round on strangers was hard enough. But to do it on your friend's brother was a whole other matter. However, Sarah, who had been assigned to look after Roddy, told her his body was in a terrible state and he winced every time they had to move him.

She stood for a moment just staring at him, and suddenly his eyes opened. Opened was perhaps the wrong word, as he couldn't open them much because of the swelling.

'Where am I? Are you an angel?'

'You're in the hospital Roddy. I'm Mary, not an angel.'

She smiled kindly at him as she said this.

'Mary Hepworth?'

'Yes. I'm a nurse here.'

'Well, thank you for looking after me, Mary. I'm afraid I wasn't very kind to you the last time we met.'

'Don't you worry about that now, Roddy. How are you feeling? Donald can't come to see you as you're not allowed visitors and has asked me if I could find out how you are.'

'That's kind of you. Tell him I'm okay, will you? I know he'll be worried sick about me.'

'I hope you don't mind me asking, but what happened to you?'

Roddy looked around before replying.

'The police aren't here, are they?'

'No.'

89

'Well, I don't know if Donald told you. I was seeing a Catholic girl called Theresa, and her father didn't want her to marry a Protestant. He had warned me off, but I needed to see her one last time and he caught us.'

'But why don't you tell the police and have him arrested? You are seriously injured. The man must be a brute.'

'He is, but I wouldn't want to cause more trouble for Theresa, and it wouldn't be fair to her family. They're not well off and he's the main breadwinner. If they sent him to jail, I don't know how Mrs Dunlop would feed and clothe the children.'

Roddy's compassion for the plight of Theresa's family surprised Mary. She had always considered him a selfish man who was only out for himself. Perhaps she had been wrong about him.

CHAPTER THIRTY-THREE

He woke up to the face of an angel, looking down at him. He thought for a moment he must be dead and wondered what had happened to him. But then he remembered. Theresa's father had battered him outside St Peter's hall. His stomach knotted as he remembered the way he had run towards him, fists flying and boots ready for kicking into him.

'Get away from my daughter or I'll kill you,' he had yelled.

Before he knew what was happening, Mr Dunlop grabbed Theresa by the hair and pulled her away from him. She screamed in agony and almost fell to the ground. He remembered seeing red and lashed out at the man. He wasn't afraid of some Irish navvy, but he realised now he should have been. Just out of the pub and full of hatred towards this upstart, he had no chance. The man grabbed him and threw him to the ground and before he knew what was happening; he was kicking into him and the pain was excruciating. He wasn't sure if the screams he could hear were his or Theresa's before he blacked out.

Losing a fight was an unfamiliar experience for him and his face grew red with shame under the swelling and bruising he had sustained. But worse than the injuries Mr Dunlop had caused him, was the memory of how he had hauled Theresa by the hair away from him. Luckily, Donald had been there and caught her before she fell to the ground. He hoped she was safe and that her father hadn't taken his anger out on her too. He vaguely remembered being lifted into an ambulance, but everything after that was a blank until now.

As he squinted at the girl through his puffy, bruised eyes, he couldn't help thinking how beautiful she looked. Her honey-coloured hair was tucked neatly under her nurse's cap, and her blue eyes were gazing anxiously down at him. She made him feel safe and warm.

'Where am I? Are you an angel?'

'You're in the hospital Roddy. I'm Mary, not an angel.'

She smiled kindly at him as she said this.

'Mary Hepworth?'

'Yes. I'm a nurse here.'

'Well, thank you for looking after me, Mary. I'm afraid I wasn't very kind to you the last time we met.'

'Don't you worry about that now, Roddy. How are you feeling? Donald can't come to see you as you're not allowed visitors and asked me if I could find out how you are.'

'That's kind of you. Tell him I'm okay, will you? I know he'll be worried sick about me.'

He wondered how Donald was and what had happened to him after he had blacked out. Had Mr Dunlop realised he was his brother and attacked him, too? But then if he had, he would be in the next bed to him, and Mary wouldn't be talking about him being unable to visit, so he must be all right.

When Mary told him the police weren't waiting to question him, he was relieved. He would need to think up a plausible story to protect Theresa's father, as much as he loathed the man. The police arrived later that day and questioned him. He didn't need to feign weakness to avoid their questions; he was genuinely in agonising pain. The doctor had told him he had bruised ribs and multiple contusions, the medical word for bruises, Mary explained to him. She had brought him a mirror to show him his face, and it had shaken him when he saw the extent of his injuries. His pride had taken a beating as well as his body, and he wondered if he would ever recover. He hated the knot of fear in his stomach when he remembered the pain as the man's boots kicked into his head and body repeatedly, even after he was down.

'Hello, Mr Macdonald. I'm Sergeant Smith from Partick Police Station. Are you able to answer our questions today? You weren't in any fit state the last time I saw you.'

'I'm not sure, Sergeant. Everything's hazy.'

'That's not surprising. Your head got a right kicking. Do you know the man who attacked you?'

'No. He was a stranger to me.'

92

'The priest told us it was Patrick Dunlop from Govan who did it. He said you were getting too friendly with his daughter Theresa.'

'I think the priest and this Patrick Dunlop must have thought I was someone else, as I don't know any Theresa Dunlop.'

He felt like Peter denying Jesus, but he didn't want to get her father into trouble in case he ended up in jail. And then where would her family be? There were a lot of mouths to feed in that house.

'Well, it's a peculiar business that a man would batter the hell out of a stranger for no reason. We've arrested him anyway, as the priest is a witness.'

'Look Sergeant, I don't know the man and I don't know any Theresa Dunlop, so I would prefer that you didn't press any charges. I want nothing to do with the man or his family. I just want to forget what happened. Can't you let him off with a caution?'

'We could if that's what you want. It would save us a lot of bother getting witness statements and taking him to court.'

'I'm a student at the University, Sergeant and it may cause bother for me if they find out I was involved in a fight. I would rather just forget the whole thing and get on with my life. I've learned my lesson. I won't be going dancing at St Peter's again.'

So, the Sergeant agreed to let the matter rest, and he never went back to St Peter's. A letter from Theresa arrived about a month after the incident, thanking him for not pressing charges against her father. She also told him she was going to America. Her father thought it would be best to remove her from temptation by sending her to his brother, who lived in Philadelphia. She told him she would never forget him and hoped he would have a happy life. This period in his life had a sobering effect on him and he tried to be less hot-headed in his dealings with people. He also changed his opinion about Mary Hepworth. Perhaps he shouldn't blame her for what her mother did, as he certainly didn't blame Theresa for what her father had done to him.

CHAPTER THIRTY-FOUR

Donald sent me a telegram, telling me Roddy had been assaulted and was in hospital. He didn't know how serious it was, but Roddy had been unconscious when the ambulance picked him up. It was plain that Donald was distressed to have sent a telegram, so I decided right then to visit Glasgow for a few days and bring Roddy home with me. But who would want to attack Roddy? Was it someone he knew, or had he just been in the wrong place at the wrong time? A big city like Glasgow could be a rough place and I had read in the papers about the razor gangs that operated there. Had he got caught up in a fight with one of those gangs? Worry for my son gripped me as memories of Roderick's last days came into my mind. I couldn't bear to lose my son, but if I were to lose him, I needed to be with him. I started praying to God to let him live and sent a telegram back to Donald, saying I would leave for Glasgow on the next boat. My mother said she would look after Heather for me.

When I arrived in Glasgow, Donald was waiting. I burst into tears when I saw him.

'How is he, Donald? Tell me he's still alive.'

'He's still alive, Ma, and the doctors have said he's going to be fine. I haven't seen him myself yet as they only allow visitors on a Wednesday during the week. But Mary tells me he's got a few cracked ribs and has multiple contusions, which means he's badly bruised. But he'll live.'

I laughed through my tears with relief. My boy was going to be okay. He was going to live. Donald put his arms around me, and we hugged like we hadn't done in a long time. What a comfort to feel close to him again. When the relief had worn off, and we were sitting in a café having a cup of tea, I questioned him.

'What happened, Donald? Surely Roddy's not involved with these razor gangs I've read about.'

'Don't be daft, Ma. It was Theresa's father who did it.'

'Theresa's father? I don't understand. I thought Roddy had decided there was no future with that girl and had finished with her.'

'Yes, you're right, but he hadn't told Theresa of his decision and we went along to the club they used to go to on the off chance that he might see her. It was when he was talking to her that her father attacked him.'

'He must be a brute of a man, to beat someone up so viciously that they end up in hospital. I warned Roddy not to get involved with that girl and I know I shouldn't say it, but I was right. Your father would have turned in his grave if he had married a Catholic.'

'Calm down, Ma. The main thing is Roddy's okay.'

'Well, I hope that man ends up in jail for what he did.'

'According to Mary, he's not planning to press charges. He doesn't want to cause Theresa's family any more trouble because of him. You know how difficult it is for people just now. If Mr Dunlop lost his job, it would be his family who would suffer.'

'How come Mary knows so much?' I couldn't help the churlish way I asked, but that was a couple of times he had mentioned Mary and she seemed to know more about Roddy than anyone else. That didn't sit well with me.

'She's working in the men's ward where they took Roddy. I asked her to look out for him and let me know how he was, so she was doing me a favour. I was told I couldn't visit him until Wednesday, which is today. So, you'll be glad to know you'll get in to see him.'

When we went up to the hospital that evening, it shocked us both to see the state Roddy was in. He tried to smile when he saw us, but his face was so badly bruised, and his lips so swollen it looked more like a grimace. I hugged him fiercely, but had to let go when he winced with pain.

'Let me go *Mathair*, my ribs can't take your affection.'

Although he tried to make light of his injuries, I knew from the way he clung to me when I hugged him that what happened had affected him more than he was letting on. My poor boy. How I hated that man for what he had done to him.

We were chatting away, and I was telling him about Archie and Flora and their new baby, when a nurse came up. Donald immediately stood up, and I knew at once it was Mary. She had certainly changed since the last time I had seen her and was now a beautiful young woman.

'Hello Auntie Chrissie,' she said, using the name she used to call me when she was a girl. I felt a lump in my throat. There was something about her that reminded me of Heather, and I felt a frisson of fear. What if she met Heather, and through some kind of sixth sense, realised they were half-sisters? I told myself not to be daft, but when I looked at Donald's face, I knew he was smitten. The girl was going to be in our lives for the foreseeable future, I was sure, so she was bound to meet Heather at some point, regardless of my fear.

1933

SECRETS AND LIES

CHAPTER THIRTY-FIVE

It was the day of his graduation, and Roddy was feeling very chuffed with himself. A First in law. Not bad for a boy from the *heilans,* as the Glaswegians called the highlands. He was now in a grand position to secure a place with an eminent law firm to serve his apprenticeship. Katie's friend Maude had agreed to help by putting the word around her contacts to find out what was available. He wanted to specialise in criminal law and fancied himself waxing lyrical in the courtroom on behalf of his clients. Professor Nicholson said he certainly had the skills to do that. But before he started working, he was looking forward to having a break after his graduation. He planned to motorcycle around the British Isles and see as many places as he could. Parts of Scotland he had never seen, England and Wales, beckoned.

His mother and sister were coming down from North Uist for his big day and he was looking forward to seeing them. He hadn't been home for nearly a year, preferring to stay in Glasgow for the Christmas/New Year holidays. His mother had written him a lovely letter when he told her his news, saying how proud she was of him. His thoughts drifted to his mother and how much her life had changed since he had left the island in 1923. She was a widow and mother to Heather, the baby that his father had never got to see. His eyes welled up with tears when he thought of his father. How he wished he was coming to his graduation, too. He so wanted him to know he had worked hard and was making the best of the chance his father had given him. He knew how ashamed he had been that time he and his mother found out he had been bullying Donald. When he thought about it, he was ashamed and relieved that he and Donald were close again.

Just then, Donald walked in as if he had known Roddy was thinking about him.

'Are you all right Roddy? You look as if you're going to blubber, but this isn't a day for tears. It's a day to celebrate.'

'I was just thinking of Father. Do you think he would be proud of me?'

The look Donald gave him told him his lack of confidence had surprised him, as he was rarely unsure of himself. His reward for showing his true feelings was a hearty slap on the back and words of encouragement.

'Of course, he would have been proud of you. You're the first one in our family to go to University and to get a First in Law is extraordinary. You're a bright spark, big brother. Even I'm proud of you.'

Roddy choked back his tears and, in a manly attempt to cover up his feeling, gave him a shove and told him to get ready.

'Mother will need you to show her and Heather where to go and I need to get all gowned up to receive my degree.'

But his heart was warm as he left his brother to get ready and made his way to the University to collect his gown.

The rest of the day went by in a blur. First, he and the other graduands went to the University Chapel for a service of thanksgiving. They then made their way to the grand hall where the Rector was waiting to tap them on the head with the mortar board and hand over the paper scroll that confirmed he was now a *Legum Baccalaureus* or, in layman's terms, a Bachelor of Laws. He would then be ready to begin his journey into the world of law. After the ceremony was over, there were strawberries and sherry served in the quadrangle. Everyone wandered around hugging and clapping each other on the back and trying to find their loved ones.

The first person he saw was Mary. She looked quite beautiful, dressed as she was in a floral summer dress with her honey-coloured hair hanging loose beneath a jaunty straw hat. She was looking a little lost among the throng and he made his way over to her quickly, not wishing her to feel uncomfortable.

'Mary! Mary!' he called.

As she turned at the sound of her name, her eyes lit up when she saw him. He reflected again on how things had changed between them.

'Hello, Roddy. My, you do look handsome in your gown. I can just see you strutting around the courtroom in it.'

'I hope so, Mary.'

Just then, he heard his name being called and turned to see his mother, Heather, and Donald, waving.

'Is that your little sister with your mother?'

'Yes, that's Heather. She's a wee beauty, isn't she?'

'Yes, she is. Whose side of the family does she take after, do you think?'

'Well, I think she has Uncle Johnny's hair; thick, black, and wild, but she has my father's blue eyes. Not much of my mother in her though, but she loves the bones of that lassie.'

There were hugs all round when they reached them. He noticed that Donald and Mary's hug lasted a bit longer than you'd expect between two friends. It made him wonder again whether their friendship was growing into something else. He also noticed that his mother only gave Mary a short hug compared to the others. She wasn't family, of course, but his mother still held a grudge against the Hepworths. Even though Donald wasn't related to her by blood, as far as his mother was concerned, he was her son. How would she react if a romance sprouted up between Donald and Mary and she became connected to the family of the woman who had done so much harm to her family?

Heather interrupted his thoughts by pulling at his hand.

'Roddy, Roddy, do you like my dress? Mammy has let me wear some of her lipstick.'

'Well, don't you look pretty, Heather? Thank you for coming to see me today. Let's celebrate.'

And off they all went to the restaurant where Katie and Maude would join them for a celebratory lunch.

CHAPTER THIRTY-SIX

When Mary saw Heather with Chrissie, her breath caught in her throat. The way the little girl ran up to Roddy, asking him if he liked her dress, reminded her so much of that day when Uncle Johnny had gone to Canada. She remembered how her mother had sent her over to talk to the boys while she had a quiet word with him. What had her mother told him? She remembered now that he was crying when she ran back to show him her dress. Why had he been so upset? It was the beginning of her mother's erratic behaviour, so she wondered what her mother had said to affect him so badly. When she looked at Heather, who was now the age she must have been around that time, she realised how much it was for a young girl to bear. She couldn't imagine Chrissie allowing anything like that to happen to Heather. She had always liked Auntie Chrissie and had hated it when she found out how much her mother had tried to hurt her and her family.

She was now working in the gynaecological ward and was finding some of the work quite harrowing. Only two days ago, a young woman came in suffering from what they thought was a miscarriage, but it turned out she had tried to end the pregnancy herself. She had poured several pots of boiling water into a tin bath in her mother's kitchen, sat in it, and then inserted a knitting needle inside herself. When the porters brought her up on a trolley, blood and blisters from the scalding hot water covered her body. Her screams of agony were horrendous, and it took Mary all her time to remain calm and help the staff nurse clean her up and give her pain relief. The poor girl didn't survive and as Mary prepared her for the porters to take to the mortuary, she wondered what had made her so desperate.

Staff nurse was unusually kind to her that afternoon and explained that the stigma of getting pregnant out with marriage was still huge.

'You'll find out, Mary, from working in this ward that it happens more often than you think, and women will do anything to preserve their reputations. But not just unmarried women go to such

101

lengths, women who already have too many children and can't afford any more will use similar methods.'

She was finding it hard to get the young woman out of her head, and memories of her mother kept intruding into her thoughts. So she needed to force herself to wear a smile when Roddy spotted her in the throng gathering in the quadrangles. It was a big day for him, and she had to admit he looked very dashing in his gown. He would make a grand lawyer one day, she was sure. But it was Donald she wanted to see; her friend that she could tell anything to. When he arrived, Donald gave her a hug, and she clung to him a little longer than necessary. Still upset by what had happened at work, she liked the warm, safe feeling of being in his arms. He, of course, immediately sensed there was something bothering her.

'Are you alright, Mary?' he asked, his eyes full of concern.

'Yes, I'm fine. Now you're here, Donald. I've had a rough few days on the ward and am feeling a little washed-out. There's something I want to talk to you about, but not now. This is Roddy's big day, so let's get on with the celebrations.'

Although the food served looked inviting, Mary found she had no appetite, so only pushed it around her plate and took the occasional nibble. Chrissie looked at her, but didn't make any comment, for which Mary was grateful. She was in no mood to be the centre of attention and have people ask her what was wrong. It was evening by the time they finished their meal, and everyone was cheery as the waiters had served champagne and wine with the food. Even she and Donald had indulged a little, so perhaps that explained what happened later.

Chrissie, Heather, Katie, and Maude made their way to the subway to go back to Cessnock, while Roddy went to Curlers, a popular public house for students. Although he invited Donald and Mary along, they declined, so this left Mary alone with Donald at last. Before making their way back to the nurses' home, they took an evening stroll through the Botanic Gardens. It was busy with evening strollers like themselves, enjoying the warm weather and the stunning array of flowers in full bloom at this time of year.

'Do you want to tell me now what's upset you so much?' he asked her when they took a seat on a bench in a little secluded section of the garden, one of their favourite places to sit when in the park.

She wondered how he would take what she was going to tell him as it affected not only her family, but his too.

CHAPTER THIRTY-SEVEN

She gave him a shortened version of what had happened with the young woman who had died in the ward, but then told him the other reason she was so upset.

'You see, Donald, I didn't know that women would take boiling baths when they were trying to stop themselves from having a baby. But when I think about my mother's strange behaviour before she had her breakdown, I remember she was always taking hot baths.'

He said nothing, just nodded, waiting for her to continue.

'It's making me think that perhaps my mother wasn't mad. That perhaps she was telling the truth when she said she'd had a baby.'

'But who could she have had a baby with?'

'She didn't say directly, but I think it was with Uncle Johnny, as she kept saying the father was in Canada and she had to let him know. Uncle Johnny used to come to our house quite a lot, and she said to me he might become my daddy one day.'

'Yes, I remember you telling me that, Mary. But Uncle Johnny married Janet. Surely he wouldn't have got your mother pregnant and then left her.'

'I don't know Donald. But I hate to think that my mother had a baby, and they took it from her. No wonder she was ill. If you and I were to make a baby together, Donald, I think I should die if anyone tried to take it away from me.'

She suddenly realised what she had said and felt her face grow hot, but Donald's next words made her wonder if he had heard her.

'Oh Mary, I can't believe Uncle Johnny would leave her like that. He must not have known. And you're right. It would be so unfair if what your mother said was true and nobody believed her. That could send a person mad. I'm seeing my ma tomorrow, so I'll ask her if she knows anything about a baby. What do you plan to do?'

'I don't know. It's not something I want to raise with my mother in a letter. I think I shall try to visit my grandma when I next get a holiday and see what she can tell me.'

'She may not tell you the truth. Look what happened to me. I only found out I wasn't Chrissie and Roderick's son because of my real father. He wanted an heir after being injured in the war, so I was it.'

She took his hand and squeezed it. He squeezed it back and looked at her fondly. 'I think you could do with a hug, Mary.'

She gladly went into his embrace and rested her head on his shoulder. Suddenly feeling overwhelmed, she sobbed as if her heart were breaking. His arms tightened round her, and he hushed her, gently patting her on the back. Then she felt his lips in her hair and looked up. Their eyes met. He brushed away her tears with his fingertips and stroked her cheek.

'May I kiss you, Mary?'

She raised her face to his and answered yes without speaking. When his lips brushed hers lightly, she thought she was going to faint.

'I think if we were to make a baby together and someone took it from us, I would die too, Mary,' he said, suddenly returning to what she had said to him before their kiss.

'Oh, Donald.'

'I love you, Mary. I didn't realise it until now. I thought we were just friends, but friends don't kiss like we just did, do they?'

She shook her head, unable to speak. Her heart was thumping in her chest, and she longed to feel his lips on hers again,

He put his hand on the back of her neck and drew her to him. She could smell a hint of lemon from the oil in his hair and hoped her breath smelled fresh. As before, his lips brushed hers gently and then it was as if he were exploring her mouth, as he leaned in towards her and his tongue brushed against hers. She tingled as his hand stroked her ear on its way down to her neck and his lips fully covered hers. Her body responded in a way she didn't know existed and it was Donald who drew back.

105

'Mary, oh Mary,' he gasped. 'You're so beautiful. But we must wait until we are married.'

She agreed with him but wished so much that they could continue to kiss and to feel these new feelings he had awakened in her. But the park was busy, and people were looking at them behaving so wantonly as they passed by.

'You're right Donald, we must wait until we are married. I don't want to end up like that poor girl.'

Donald looked hurt.

'Mary, I would never make a baby with you and then abandon you. Don't you know that?'

'I'm sorry, Donald. Of course, I do. But anything can happen. Look at your mother. Uncle Roderick died and left her on her own with a baby. They were married, but what if they hadn't been? She would have been in the same position as my mother.'

Before she realised what was happening, Donald knelt on the path and took her hands in his.

'Will you do me the honour of becoming my wife, Mary Hepworth? I love you with all my heart and I want us to be together forever.'

Her breath caught in her throat, and tears welled in her eyes.

'Oh Donald, yes, yes. I want nothing more than to be your wife.'

She pulled him up, and they joyously embraced each other to the sound of applause from the passers-by who had gathered when they saw Donald getting down on one knee.

When they arrived at the nurses' home, they shared a tender, sweet kiss that she didn't want to end. But they hastily separated, as the door opened and the housekeeper stepped out of the house to go home.

'Now, now, Nurse Hepworth. This isn't the place to be getting fresh with your boyfriend. Better move away before Sister Tutor sees you. If she does, you'll get no more leave this month.'

Donald murmured sorry to Mrs Munro, as she made her way out of the grounds, but then turned to Mary with a huge grin.

'Oh, my word, Mary. I hope I haven't got you into trouble.'

She had never seen him look so happy or speak so mischievously and she trembled with desire for this man who was to be her future husband.

'Feeling your lips on mine is worth any trouble I might get into,' she whispered, gazing up into his eyes, inviting him to kiss her again. His lips met hers once more, and their bodies melted into one another. She felt dizzy and pushed him gently away as the image of Sister MacFarlane came into her mind. 'But it would mean I wouldn't be able to see you again for a long time if Sister Tutor saw us.'

'Okay Mary. I better go. I couldn't bear it if I didn't see you again soon.'

She went inside and lingered at the door, waving to him until he turned the corner and was out of sight. Her heart was full of joy. Donald loved her and had asked her to be his wife. She couldn't wait to tell Cynthia.

CHAPTER THIRTY-EIGHT

Donald walked with a spring in his step as he made his way back to his digs in Partick. For the first time in his life, he had taken a chance. He had kissed Mary and had asked her to marry him, and she had agreed. How could a person's life change in an instant like that? He couldn't quite believe it. The sense of excitement and overwhelming happiness made him notice what a beautiful evening it was. The sun dappled through the leafy trees that grew in the middle of his street and the song thrushes sung their sweet evening chorus. He wanted to write a poem for Mary and to skip like a child again, although he recognised he had never been one to do much skipping when he was young. After he found out Colin Donaldson was his father and Roddy turned against him, he found it hard to be spontaneous and light-hearted.

When he arrived home, Jimmy was sitting in his wheelchair at the front door of the close enjoying a smoke. His life had changed so much since the hunger march last year. Although he had lost a leg in the war, he had still managed to shuffle around with his peg leg. But after the beating he had received from the mounted police in London, he was bedridden and needed a wheelchair to move around. It had been an enormous change for him and Annie, who no longer worked so that she could look after him. The dirty means test, as Jimmy called it, had been inflicted on them when Annie tried to claim the unemployment benefit. It was shameful how those officials treated them, and he and Roddy had felt justified in telling lies when they asked how much rent they paid for their room. He sometimes wondered where Jimmy's daughter was as he thought she might have come home to see her father after he had been injured, but she never had. And he didn't like to ask in case it upset Jimmy that she hadn't come home.

'Hello there Donald. How was the graduation? Come and have a cup of tea. Annie has baked some scones.'

The heat in the kitchen was overwhelming, and Donald had to wipe his face with his handkerchief.

'Feeling the heat, son. Well, let me tell you, this is nothing to the heat we had to endure in the trenches on those hot summer days in France during the war.'

Donald smiled to himself. If he wasn't talking politics, Jimmy could always find an excuse to talk about the war and, if his stories were to be believed, he was a hero. This day, however, his story took a different tack, and it was to be the beginning of an enormous change in Donald's life. Instead of talking about himself, Jimmy talked about a man he fought beside that he would never forget.

'He was a Cree Indian who came from Saskatchewan in Canada and went by the name of Henry Norwest. At first, none of us were sure of him, because he was different, you know?'

He pulled a face, and Donald wondered if Jimmy knew he had Cree blood in him. He shivered slightly despite the heat and felt the familiar knot of anxiety he always got in his stomach when anyone asked him about his family. But as Jimmy continued to speak, Donald realised he was giving him a clue that the man didn't look like them. Donald nodded to show he understood as he did understand. He knew what it was like to be different. The sound of Flora McIntyre and some of the other children dancing round him, calling him a bastard and a Red Indian, still haunted him sometimes.

'But, you know Donald, I never met a nicer man nor a better sniper than Henry Norwest. We fought together at Vimy Ridge, Passchendaele, and Amiens until a German sniper shot him. He's buried in France with all the other brave soldiers who fought in that terrible war. I hope they gave him a medal of honour for his efforts.'

Jimmy's eyes glistened with unshed tears, and Donald's heart went out to him. How awful to fight for your country and lose a leg, only to be hounded by the means test when you made a claim for money to live on.

The sound of the front door opening and Roddy's voice singing out one of the latest popular tunes abruptly interrupted their conversation. This meant he couldn't ask Jimmy anything more

109

about Henry Norwest. But it didn't matter. He knew something in him had changed from hearing the old man's story.

'I better go, Jimmy. That's my brother back from celebrating his graduation and it sounds as if he's had rather a lot to drink.'

'Quite right. Make hay while the sun shines. Things aren't looking so good in the world right now, what with the depression and inflation in Germany. We might be at war again soon for all we know.'

Donald shuddered at the thought. He couldn't imagine himself ever taking up arms against anyone.

CHAPTER THIRTY-NINE

Roddy and Donald came to visit Heather and me the day following Roddy's graduation. We were both tired, as Maude had put records on the gramophone when we returned to Cessnock after the celebrations. We had all danced until it was time for Heather to go to bed. But our tiredness didn't mar our delight at seeing the boys. Not that they were boys any longer; they had both grown into handsome men in their own way. My delight didn't last long, however, when Donald asked if he could speak to me privately. I immediately wondered if Mary had noticed something about Heather that had given the game away about her parentage. While what Donald told me was linked to Heather, it was clear he and Mary had no suspicions that she was Bunty's daughter rather than mine.

'So, Donald, what do you want to talk to me about? I hope there's nothing wrong.'

'No, Ma. Everything is right for once in my life.'

I looked at him closely when he said this and realised that what he said was true. His eyes were bright, and he had a relaxed air about him I had never seen since he was a young child. What on earth could have made such a change in him? It had to be a woman. Was it Mary? Had they become more than friends?

'Well, tell me. What's happened? I can see you're happy, Donald, and it warms my heart to see you like this. Are you in love?'

'Yes, Ma, I am in love. I'm in love with Mary. We told each other yesterday, and I've asked her to be my wife.'

Although his news didn't surprise me, I felt a hard lump in my throat and the words of congratulations that I should have spoken stuck there. His face fell and I could see my reaction disappointed him.

'Well, say something, Ma. I know it's awkward after what Mary's mother did to our family, but she's nothing like her mother. Bunty lives in Canada now, so you need never see her again.'

111

'Och Donald, I'm sorry. I'm just surprised, that's all. I knew you and Mary were close friends, but I didn't realise you were more than that. Come here, my boy. I'm delighted for you. If Mary makes you happy, then that makes me happy. You've not had an easy time of it in your young life, so you deserve all the happiness in the world.'

He eagerly came into my arms, and we clung to each other, he no doubt with relief and me with fear at what this might mean for the secret I carried.

'I also have other things to speak to you about, Ma. I hope what I'm about to say won't bring back unhappy memories for you, but I must ask you for my sake and for Mary's.'

'Mary's?'

'Yes. It's about her mother. She says the doctors in the asylum where they locked Bunty up after she moved from North Uist, kept her in for about a year. Apparently, they decided she was still ill as she kept telling people she'd had a baby and that she had to let the father know. She said the father lived in Canada.'

I just stared at him. I couldn't believe what I was hearing.

'She told Mary this same story, when she was eventually released, but Mary didn't believe her as her grandma told her it wasn't true. But recently she's discovered that women who don't want to have a baby take hot baths.'

'Hot baths? How does she know that?'

I was stalling for time, afraid of what he was about to ask me.

'She's working in the gynaecology ward and had a patient who died because of it.'

'So, what's that got to do with what you want to ask me?'

'She remembers her mother used to take hot baths all the time. So, it's making her wonder if her mother did have a baby and they took it from her. I said I would ask you if you knew anything.'

I rose from the chair and walked over to the window. I needed time to think about what I would say to him. Was it time to tell the truth or to keep lying?

112

'She also wonders if the father was Uncle Johnny as he used to visit them a lot and Bunty told Mary that he might become her daddy one day. Do you remember I told you and Father that?'

I turned to him. I had decided to keep lying.

'Yes, I remember, Donald. Bunty also said something like that to me when she was in the Poorhouse, but I didn't take her seriously. She was very ill.'

'So, you don't know if she had a baby then?'

'No, I'm sorry. I don't. What will Mary do now?'

'She's going home to Manchester next month for a holiday and will ask her grandma, but as I told her, she may not tell the truth. People keep secrets, don't they?'

I didn't answer. We both knew he was talking about Roderick and me, not telling him the truth about his birth.

'Well, I hope she finds a satisfactory explanation. Shall we go back downstairs now and tell everyone your joyful news? A wedding in the family. I can hardly believe it. When do you plan to wed?'

'We've only just decided we love each other, Ma. Give us a chance. But before we go downstairs, I want to ask you one last thing.'

I had to stop myself from sighing. What now?

'I was talking to my landlord, Jimmy Thompson, and he spoke to me about the war and about a Cree soldier he fought beside. Apparently, he was very brave and a wonderful sniper who saved many lives.'

'I didn't know Indians fought in the war. But I suppose they have the same rights and obligations as other Canadian citizens.'

'He said the man's name was Norwest, and I had a vague recollection of you telling me that Heather's mother was called Lily Norwest, but I couldn't be sure. I just wanted to check with you.'

I felt relieved. This had nothing to do with Heather, thank goodness.

'Yes, you're right Donald. That was her name. Do you think this soldier could be her relative?'

113

'I don't know, but I would love to find out. For the first time, I feel something rather than shame about my heritage.'

'I'm glad you feel like that, Donald. You've nothing to be ashamed of. Heather was a lovely young woman that any boy would have been proud to have as their mother.'

We hugged again, and I felt so relieved for him. Carrying shame all these years had marred his life. How I hoped his life would change for the better now.

'Let's go downstairs and tell everyone about you and Mary. Perhaps Maude will have a bottle of something locked away somewhere to toast this wonderful news.'

He laughed, and we walked downstairs hand in hand to the kitchen. Although I was happy for Donald, I wasn't so happy for myself and Heather. The last thing I wanted was any connection with Bunty's family, but there was nothing I could do about it. Our future was in God's hands now.

CHAPTER FORTY

Roddy wondered why Donald wished to speak to his mother privately and felt a little excluded when they left the room to have a chat. When they came back into the room after their chat and his mother announced that Donald and Mary were going to be married, he felt even more left out. Why hadn't Donald told him first? He was his brother, and they shared the same room, for God's sake. Surely it wasn't too much to ask. Then he remembered he had been rather the worse for wear last night after being in Curlers with his friends, so perhaps it wouldn't have been the best time. But he could have told him about it this morning on the way over to visit his mother. Feeling annoyed that he hadn't done so, his thoughts became disparaging. How had Donald plucked up the courage to declare his feelings and pop the question to Mary? He wasn't exactly the bravest of people and had practically no experience of girls.

'Donald, you dark horse. You never told me you and Mary were walking out together.'

'We weren't. We were just friends. Until yesterday,' Donald said, blushing brightly.

Roddy felt a surge of blood to his groin as he remembered the passionate kissing he and Theresa had exchanged on the day they declared their love for each other. Feeling jealous, he pushed away the image of Donald and Mary engaging in such behaviour. How lucky Donald was to have met someone who loved him as much as he loved her. He could see from his mother's face that she was pleased for Donald. Even though it was the last thing she wanted, she clearly wasn't going to place any obstacles in the way of him finding happiness with Mary.

As he looked at her smiling face, all the old resentment resurfaced. She would have abandoned him if he had married Theresa. Yet here she was, prepared to accept a girl whose mother had been responsible for her husband's death just to please Donald. It had always been the same. She thought more of Donald than of him, her own son.

115

'So, Mother, you're happy to let Donald marry the daughter of the woman who killed my father.'

Before Chrissie could say anything, Donald intervened.

'What's got into you Roddy? I thought you liked Mary now and accepted she wasn't to blame for what her mother did. I was hoping you would be my Best Man, but if you still feel like that about Mary, then I shall have to ask someone else.'

'Who else would you ask? You have no friends, Donald.'

'That's enough Roddy. Don't speak to your brother like that.'

'He's not my brother. Remember? He's the bastard child of Colin Donaldson and Heather, Bunty's half-sister. His relationship with Mary is almost incestuous.'

Everyone was staring at him, open-mouthed. He knew what he was saying was shocking, but he felt incapable of stopping himself, and was relieved when Maude intervened.

'Right, Roddy, you need to leave my house now. This conversation is not acceptable. You're upsetting Heather.'

It troubled Roddy to see his little sister in tears, and he took a step towards her. But she recoiled from him, threw herself at her mother, who put her arms around her protectively. Feeling foolish and rebuked, he collected his coat and made his way out of the house. He was at a loss to understand why he had become so angry and said such hurtful words. Poor Donald. He had spoiled his special announcement.

CHAPTER FORTY-ONE

When Roddy left the house, we all stood in stunned silence until Heather spoke in a whisper.

'What's a bastard *Mamaidh*?'

I looked at her little face, tear stained and scared. I was going to have to tell her about Donald, but not now. How long were these secrets going to keep resurfacing? Had I done the wrong thing by pretending Heather was my daughter? Was it another secret that would surface one day and haunt us for the rest of our lives? But how could I tell her the truth now?

'It's a bad word, Heather.'

'But why did he call Donald a bad word?'

'I don't know, *mo graidh*. Perhaps he's anxious about starting work. It's a huge thing when you have to grow up and start earning a living. You'll know all about it when you grow up. Now let's go out for some fresh air. A walk in Bellahouston Park is just what we need.'

Fortunately, Heather didn't pursue it any further and went to put her outdoor shoes on.

When she left the room, I went over to Donald and gave him a hug.

'I'm so sorry, Donald. I don't know what's got into him.'

'I don't know either, but I'm going to find out. I can't believe he spoke like that when we were guests in Maude's house and in front of little Heather. He's gone too far this time.'

'What are you going to do?' asked Katie, who had been silent throughout the whole thing.

'I'm going to cool off before I talk to him. That's the first thing. I can't believe he was so out of control like that. After the beating from Mr Dunlop, he seemed to calm down and think before he spoke. But that all went out the window today. I can only think something else is upsetting him. As Ma says, maybe he's just anxious about graduating and finding work.'

'Well, I can tell you Donald, if he is to become a lawyer, he will need to keep his temper in check. He wouldn't get away with that kind of behaviour in court,' said Maude.

I knew she'd been helping Roddy find a placement to begin his training after the holidays, and I prayed to God that what happened today wouldn't affect that.

'That's me ready, *Mamaidh*,' said Heather, coming back into the room. 'Can we play on the swings?'

'Yes, of course.'

Thank goodness children seem able to put unpleasant things to the back of their minds and just live in the moment. However, while we were out, Heather came back to the earlier conversation and asked me again why Roddy had called Donald a bad word. So, I told her in the simplest terms I could about Donald.

'Donald's *mamaidh*, Heather, died when he was born. She wasn't married to his father, so your *dadaidh*, Roderick, and I adopted him and told people he was our son. People don't like when a baby is born to unmarried parents, so they refer to the child as illegitimate and sometimes the word that Roddy said.'

'Am I called after Heather?'

'Yes.'

'Why?'

This was becoming more complicated than I thought.

'Because she was a lovely girl, just like you, and your *dadaidh* and I were very fond of her. Oh, look, there's an ice cream seller. Shall we go buy some?'

I always find diverting a child with food is an excellent tactic for changing the subject of an awkward conversation.

CHAPTER FORTY-TWO

Donald left the house with Chrissie and Heather and made his way along to the subway. His mind was working feverishly. He was livid with Roddy for speaking to him like that, in front of everyone. It was an insult and a slight on Mary. His news should have pleased Roddy, but it only seemed to have enraged him. Was he jealous? Was that the reason he had behaved like that? But what did he have to be jealous of? He had just graduated with an Honours Degree and was about to embark on a motorcycle adventure before beginning his law career. He was fulfilling his dreams; doing what he had always wanted to do, so he had nothing to be jealous of.

Worse than what he had said was how he had made Donald feel. He hated that his stomach had turned to mush, and no words of defence had come to him. He had felt like that little boy who Roddy used to bully so cruelly. Well, he wasn't getting away with it this time. He'd never stood up to Roddy, but he was going to stand up to him now. He remembered what Jimmy had said about the Cree soldier and somehow took courage from the courage of that unknown man. It was time for him to follow in the footsteps of his ancestors, instead of feeling ashamed and cowed.

When he got back to his digs, Roddy was waiting for him and spoke before he had time to say anything.

'I'm so sorry, Donald. I don't know what got into me. I think I was jealous.'

'Jealous? You have the world at your feet, Roddy. What have you to be jealous of?'

'I don't know. Maybe it's losing Theresa and hearing the news about you and Mary.'

He muttered his words, and his eyes glistened with unshed tears. Losing that girl had meant much more to him than he had let on, but it was no excuse for how he had behaved.

'So, because you don't have a girl to love, you feel it's okay to speak to me like a piece of dirt on your shoe. You're a self-centred ass and always have been. Well, I'm not a wee six-year-old boy that you can say what you like to Roddy. I'm a man and I won't stand for it.'

'What are you going to do?'

'I don't know, but I'm not sharing this room with you any longer. I'll ask Katie if I can stay with her and Maude until I get sorted.'

As he spoke, he pulled his suitcase from under his bed and began throwing clothes into it. He knew he was being rash, but felt he had to act. He was sick of letting people walk all over him. Jimmy was right. Sometimes you had to make a stand against oppression. Ma would be upset, but he couldn't take responsibility for what Roddy had done.

'Please don't leave, Donald. You're my brother.'

Roddy's Adam's apple was bobbing in his throat as he tried to keep his emotions in check.

'I know what I did was wrong and I'm sorry. I know I've always been a bit of an arse where you're concerned, but it doesn't mean you're not important to me. I don't want to lose you as well as Theresa.'

Donald's anger left him as he thought about what it would be like to lose Mary. He knew it would be almost impossible to bear. And did he really want to break up his relationship with his brother?

'I can only imagine how much you miss Theresa, Roddy, but I'm so disappointed in you. Your outburst upset everyone on what should have been one of the happiest days of our lives.'

'I know Donald. Tell me how I can make it up to you?'

'I need to know you don't still dislike Mary and blame her for what her mother did. I thought you had got over all that. I want you to be my Best Man but if you feel like that about Mary, then you can't be.'

'I like Mary, Donald. You know I do. I don't know why I said that. And I'm sorry for what I said about you not having friends.'

Donald laughed lightly.

'Well, it's true, but you didn't have to point it out to everyone.'

He knew he was letting his brother off the hook, but Roddy genuinely looked sorry.

120

'Look, you must apologise to Ma, Katie, and Maude. It was very difficult for them to see you behaving in that way. Maude says you won't get away with that kind of behaviour in a courtroom, so you need to get a grip. And wee Heather was so upset. You'll need to make your peace with her before she and Ma go back to North Uist tomorrow.'

'I will Donald, I will. Thank you. You're better than the best brother I could have. It will be an honour to stand beside you and Mary on your wedding day.'

They shook hands, and it was over. They were brothers again, but somehow more equal brothers than they had ever been before.

CHAPTER FORTY-THREE

Mary didn't find out what had happened between the brothers until she and Donald were on their way to Manchester to visit her grandma. She only had a week off and wanted to make the most of it. Her priority was to introduce Donald to her family and to allow him to ask for her hand in marriage. She also wanted to discover more about her mother and the fate of her child if it turned out she had been pregnant. Donald was only coming for a couple of days to ask for her hand in marriage, as he was going on a Hunger March to Edinburgh with Jimmy. Although Jimmy could no longer walk, Donald would push him in his wheelchair with the help of others in the NUWM.

She sometimes worried that Donald was turning into a Communist, although he had never told her he was a member of the party. Not that she was unsympathetic to the plight of the poor. She knew that many of the patients who came into the hospital were only there because they were destitute. They were grateful for a bath and some hot food. But she wasn't sure how she would feel about being married to a revolutionary, then smiled at the idea of Donald being one of those. He was the gentlest and kindest person she knew.

They travelled by train to Manchester. Mary's Grandma had sent them first-class tickets, which meant they enjoyed an excellent lunch and refreshments. Donald was nervous about meeting her family.

'I hope your Grandma likes me, Mary. Is it better for me to ask your Uncle Charles for your hand in marriage in the absence of your mother rather than your grandmother? I'm not sure what the protocol is.'

'I'm not sure either, but I think we can speak to my grandma informally and then you could ask Uncle Charles, just to give him his place. How does that sound?'

'It sounds perfect, Mary. You always come up with a solution.'

'I wonder how Roddy is getting on. Travelling around on that motorbike of his must be thrilling. Oh, to feel the wind in your hair and be as free as a bird.'

'Perhaps he'll take you for a ride. Would you like that?'

'Maybe. But It will be nice to see him again, won't it? He's been away for a while now.'

'Yes, he has, but to be honest, I think it's been good for us both to have a break from each other.'

'Why do you say that, Donald? I thought you got on well together.'

'We did... we do. But he behaved quite badly when I told the family that you and I were to be married. I said nothing to you at the time as I was upset and didn't want to upset you and make you think he didn't want me to marry you.'

'What happened? I hate to think of you being upset.'

She took his hand in hers, hoping he had stood up to Roddy. He could be overbearing sometimes.

'Perhaps he felt you were taking the limelight away from his big day by telling everyone you and I are getting married.'

'Perhaps, but I'm not sure. It was horrible to see him all bitter and twisted with jealousy the way he was when I was a boy. Och, but I got over it. I was quite proud of myself, actually. I threatened to move out and told him he must apologise to Chrissie and the others, which he did. He was very contrite and told me how proud he would be to stand beside us as my Best Man on our wedding day.'

"Bravo!"

'I feel so different now that you and I are to be married, but there's something I haven't told you yet. On the night I proposed, I got chatting with Jimmy when I got home, and you'll never guess what he told me.'

Mary smiled fondly at him. He was grinning from ear to ear, so it must be something special. When he told her what Jimmy had told him about Henry Norwest, she agreed it certainly was something special.

123

'And when I asked my Mother if that was Lily's name, she confirmed it was. So, it's made me even more determined to go to Canada and find out more about my ancestors. I feel so different now about my heritage. I don't feel so ashamed anymore. Does your grandmother know about my background?'

'I'm not sure. It's never come up in conversation, but Uncle Charles might know something about it, as I'm sure your mother must have told him what my mother did. Are you worried they might disapprove?'

'Not so much now, but what if they do and won't give their consent for us to be married?'

'Well, then we shall run away to Gretna Green. Nothing and nobody is going to stop us from being together, Donald.'

They sat in silence for a time, watching the scenery rushing by. The only sound was the clickity clack of the train on the lines and the occasional blast of steam from the chimney. Mary's thoughts drifted to the other reason she was going to Manchester. She wanted to find out as much as she could about her mother and the baby she said she'd had. It was good Uncle Charles was going to be there, as he would know if her mother had been pregnant and if she was, who had adopted the baby.

'I feel a little nervous, Donald, about asking my grandma and Uncle Charles about my mother. Do you think I'm doing the right thing?'

'Yes, I think you are. It's troubling you that you didn't believe your mother when she told you about having a baby, so I think it would be good for your peace of mind to find out the truth. Having said that, I don't think it'll be easy for them to tell you. Family secrets are secret for a reason, so I think your family will find it hard to be honest with you.'

'I understand what you're saying, but I can only hope that when I confront them, they'll find it hard to keep lying.'

'I hope so too, Mary.'

CHAPTER FORTY-FOUR

When they arrived in Manchester, a car was waiting to pick them up. It was a rather smart cream and brown saloon with brown leather seats. Although Donald knew Mary's family was wealthy, he hadn't thought she would have servants, as she was so down to earth. Yet here she was, looking quite comfortable about having a driver to take them home from the station. He wasn't uncomfortable. He had experienced what it was like to have servants when he lived for a brief time with his father and when Chrissie and Roderick moved into the Factor's house. It was changed days now, of course, living in digs in a Partick tenement, sharing a room with Roddy. He hoped Mary's uncle wouldn't question him too closely about his wealth and position.

'Hello, Stanley. It's good to see you,' said Mary.

'And you Miss Mary. Your grandma can't wait to see you and to meet your young man.'

'This is Donald.'

Donald held his hand out and shook the man's hand.

'I'm pleased to meet you, Stanley.'

'And me you, sir. Let me put your bags into the boot and then we'll get you home.'

'Thank you.'

On the journey out to the suburbs, Mary and Stanley chatted away amicably. She told him how much she enjoyed living in Glasgow and how her nurses' training was coming along. Fortunately, she didn't go into it in as much detail as she had with him. He said nothing for the entire journey, conscious of a queasiness in his stomach at the thought of meeting Mary's family. But he needn't have worried. Grace Adams was as down to earth as Mary and shook his hand enthusiastically in welcome.

'Hello Donald, I'm delighted to meet you. I feel as if I know you already, as Mary has talked about you many times since she came back from North Uist.'

The woman was about the same age as his granny, had silver hair and bright grey eyes, which crinkled at the side when she smiled. She was shorter than Mary and looked a little like he remembered Bunty looking when he first met her.

'I'm pleased to meet you too, Mrs Adams. Mary talks about you a lot, too.'

'Betty here will show you to your room, and we'll have dinner once you're settled.'

A petite girl with curly red hair smiled at him and asked him to follow her. His room was on the first floor. It was bright and looked out over the gardens and the gravel driveway they had driven up. Mary's grandfather must have made a lot of money in the war for the family to afford a house like this. It was despicable that some people could profit from war, while others like Jimmy ended up disabled and unemployed. Donald's queasiness disappeared, and he realised he had nothing to fear from this family. He wanted Mary's family to approve of their union, but if they didn't, he was sure Mary would still marry him. He, therefore, decided he would enjoy this brief break and get to know Mary's family. If all went well, they would become his family, too.

A gong sounded, and he went downstairs where Stanley was waiting to show him into the dining room. Mrs Adams and a man in his mid-thirties that Donald assumed was Mary's Uncle Charles were already sitting at the table.

'Sit here, beside me, Donald,' said Grace. 'This is my son, Charles. He's come up from London especially to meet you.'

'Thank you, Mrs Adams. I'm pleased to meet you, Mr Adams. It's kind of you to come all this way just for me.'

Charles smiled at him, then winked.

'I thought my presence may be required if you and Mary have come here to tell us you hope to marry.'

Donald blushed and wondered what to say, but Mary came into the room and saved him from having to answer.

'Hello everyone. Sorry I'm late. It's lovely to see you, Uncle Charles,' she said, going over and kissing him on the cheek. He rose and hugged her with obvious affection.

'Hello Mary. You look lovely tonight. I think you have a special glow about you.'

'Thank you, Uncle Charles,' she said, smiling widely and giving first her grandma and then Donald a kiss on the cheek as well.

Donald agreed with her uncle. She looked beautiful. Her blue eyes were shining, her corn-coloured hair cascaded over her shoulders and glowed against the navy blue fitted dress she was wearing. His heart missed a beat as he remembered their first kiss and that she had agreed to be his wife.

'So, Donald, tell us a bit about yourself. I don't believe in beating about the bush.'

'Oh, Charles, give the boy time to have his dinner before you begin the cross-examination,' said his mother.

'You already know that I met Donald when mummy and I lived in North Uist, so we have known each other and have been best friends forever.'

When Mary mentioned North Uist, Donald thought Charles looked a little uncomfortable. He was a little uncomfortable himself and wondered what Mary was up to talking about her mother so soon in the conversation.

'Donald and I have a family connection. Donald's mother, Heather, was my mother's half-sister, as you know, so that makes us second cousins or something like that.'

'And your father, Donald. I heard from your um guardian, Mrs Macdonald, he was the Factor on North Uist before he died.'

'That's right, Mr Adams. The Laird of North Uist is a relative of my father's family and gave my grandfather and then my father the job of Factor. I think he's hoping I might follow them, but I have no interest in doing that.'

'And what are you interested in, Donald?' asked Grace.

'I'm interested in literature, and hope to be a writer someday. I'm studying for a Master of Arts at the University of Glasgow.'

'And will that earn you a lot of money, Donald, or do you not need to worry about earning a living?'

127

'Uncle Charles, don't be so rude,' interceded Mary before Donald could answer. 'Donald will be a successful writer and I shall be a successful matron in Glasgow's Western Infirmary, where I'm now a trainee. So, we'll have plenty to live on.'

He loved that Mary was trying to protect him, but it was better to get things like this over with, so he spoke up.

'I understand why your uncle is asking me these questions, Mary. He only wants to know that I can look after you, so I don't mind answering. Unfortunately, because of the financial crash of 1929, the money I inherited from my father is less than it was. But Mary and I will still be able to live comfortably in comparison with many others during these difficult times. It won't be as grand as this, but we shall be happy.'

Charles stared at him for a moment before continuing.

'So, is this your way of asking for Mary's hand in marriage, Donald?'

Donald sensed his disapproval that he was bringing politics into the conversation and felt the need to rile him even more.

'Yes, sir. It is. But you haven't asked about my mother, so perhaps I should let you know where I come from before you consider my request.'

Charles stared at him again and then spoke.

'We already know that my uncle married a Cree Indian and that your mother was her daughter, but it's honest of you to bring the matter up. I'm sure some people would want to hide such things.'

'Yes, I was one of them until recently, even although I knew it made no difference to Mary. But that's all changed since I found out one of my ancestors was a hero in the war.'

Donald thought Grace or Charles might ask more, but Charles changed the subject.

'What does Mrs Macdonald think of the arrangement? Is she happy for you to wed Mary? How is Mrs Macdonald, by the way? She hadn't long lost her husband, and I believe was expecting his child when I last saw her. She was a great help when my sister was ill.'

Donald wondered how Charles knew his mother had been expecting a child. As far as he could remember, even he and Roddy didn't know his mother was pregnant with Heather at the time they took Bunty to the asylum.

'Chrissie is doing fine, sir. Her little girl, Heather, is now almost twelve and yes, she has given us her blessing.'

'Twelve, you say. My how the years pass. Well, Mother, what do you think? Is this boy a suitable suitor for our Mary?'

'Stop teasing him, Charles. I'm happy if Mary's happy. So, stop beating about the bush and tell him he can marry her.'

He held his breath, waiting for Charles to speak. When he answered in the affirmative, he could not resist standing up and vigorously shaking everyone's hand. He had never felt so happy and by the look on Mary's face; she was feeling the same. He was desperate to take her in his arms and kiss her, but didn't quite have the courage to do so in front of her family.

CHAPTER FORTY-FIVE

Mary's joy at her engagement to Donald didn't stop her from wanting to learn as much as possible about her mother while she was visiting. For the short time Donald was with them, she didn't get the chance to speak to her uncle or her grandma, as they were so busy. Their time was taken up with visiting Manchester during the day and attending the theatre in the evening. She only got to speak privately to her uncle on the day they saw Donald off on the train back to Glasgow. Charles was travelling back to London from the same station, but his train was later, so they went to the tearoom while they waited. It was stifling hot, despite the open windows on this warm summer day, and they decided on a cool glass of lemonade rather than tea. When the waitress had served them, they chatted, and Mary wondered how she could raise the question of her mother. But the chance arose while they were talking, and his response to her question changed everything.

'So, are you truly happy for us, Uncle Charles? Do you think Donald is the man for me?'

'Yes, of course, I am Mary. He seems a nice young man. You have your own money to live on if necessary, so we don't need to worry about that. And if he's related to the Laird of North Uist, he may come into some money in the future.'

'Money isn't everything, Uncle Charles.'

'It is if you don't have it, Mary.'

She felt ashamed of her thoughtlessness and was thankful that Donald wasn't there to hear her remark. Of course, it was everything when you had none. According to Donald, the government was doing nothing to help the poor. He said it was okay for rich people, but working people lived constantly at a subsistence level so had nothing to fall back on if the economy slumped. Then she thought of her mother. Having money didn't protect her from losing her mind and being sent to an asylum and, if she was to be believed, from having her baby taken from her. Before she took time to think about what she was saying, she blurted out the question she wanted the answer to.

'Did my mother have a baby when she was in the asylum, Uncle Charles?'

He looked shocked at her question and glanced round the tearoom to make sure there was no one they knew.

'Where did that come from? One minute we're talking about money and the next about your mother.'

'My mother told me when I was a little girl that she had had a baby, but I didn't believe her. I thought if she'd had a baby, she would have brought it home with her.'

'Have you spoken to your grandma about it?'

'Not yet. I've not really had a chance, what with getting engaged and everything.'

'But why are you asking about this now?'

'Mother has been on my mind, and I fear I've done her a disservice.'

She then told him what she had found out while working in the women's ward.

'It made me remember that when my mother's behaviour became strange, she took hot baths every night. So, it's made me wonder if she was telling the truth.'

As she waited for his answer, his face was a picture of indecision and she knew with certainty that, whatever he was about to tell her, her mother had told her the truth.

'Your mother did have a child, Mary, a little girl. But the child died. I know it's cruel to say so but, it was the best thing. Having an illegitimate child would have ruined her reputation and prevented her from ever marrying again.'

'But why did they keep her so long in the asylum? Why couldn't she just come home?'

'She kept insisting on talking about the baby and about letting the father know, so your Grandma and I thought it best to leave her there a little longer. I'm sorry for that now, but we felt it would mess up all our plans to keep her reputation intact.'

Mary found herself in tears. Her poor mother. Losing her baby and then being kept in that asylum just to cover up her disgrace.

131

She had never married again anyway, so it had all been for nothing.

'What happened to my sister's body, Uncle Charles?'

Now he looked really uncomfortable, and Mary wondered what he was about to tell her.

'People are looking at us, Mary. I think it's best if we move outside, don't you?'

She didn't care if people were looking at her, but she mopped up her tears, blew her nose with the large linen handkerchief her uncle gave her, and rose from the table. The sound of crockery and cutlery faded into the background as she made her way towards the door. All she could think about was what had happened to her mother and the baby. Distracted by her thoughts, she bumped into a man coming through the door as she was leaving, and he caught her just before she fell.

'Mary?'

She looked up to see Roddy.

'Are you alright, Mary? You look as if you've been crying.'

And before she knew what was happening, he had taken her outside, and she was in his arms sobbing as if her heart would break. It was her uncle who brought her back to the present.

'Mary. What's going on? Who is this man?'

'He's Donald's brother,' she gulped through her tears. 'Roddy, this is my Uncle Charles. He's just given me some news that's shaken me up somewhat.'

'I can see that.'

'But what are you doing here, Roddy? I thought you were motorcycling round Britain.'

'I was. I am. But I remembered that you and Donald were planning to come to Manchester for a few days and thought I might get the chance of catching up with you. I only came into the café because I needed a drink.'

'Well, thank goodness you did, young man. My train to London is due any minute now and I need to get on it, but I was worried about leaving Mary like this. Will you take care of her and see she gets home safely? Our driver is waiting outside.'

'Yes, of course, I will,' said Roddy, looking askance at Mary. She knew she would need to explain what had upset her, but given Roddy's hostility towards her mother, she wasn't sure he would understand. Feeling rather foolish now that her emotions were in check again, she waved reassuringly to her uncle as his train left.

CHAPTER FORTY-SIX

After seeing Mary to the car, where a man called Stanley was waiting for her, Roddy went to pick up his motorcycle. Mary had invited him to stay for a few days while he was in Manchester, but he didn't want to leave his bike in the city centre. He imagined the area around the station might be unsafe, as it was in other cities, and worried his Norton might become a target for thieves. The last thing he wanted was to lose it, as he still had a lot of travelling to do. While walking to where he had parked it, he thought about the man who was her Uncle Charles. The man seemed familiar, but Roddy reasoned it was unlikely he would know him if he lived in London. But there was something about him that made him feel uneasy. He wondered what he'd said that had caused Mary to cry like that.

The floral smell of her hair and the feel of her small body wrapped in his arms, shuddering with sobs, was still with him. Surely her uncle hadn't refused to approve her and Donald's engagement. He noticed a pang of something akin to pleasure at this thought and couldn't understand why. Surely he wasn't still feeling antipathy towards Mary. But when he thought of his overwhelming need to comfort her when she was weeping, he at once discounted this idea. It was puzzling, but he set it aside for now, as he needed to concentrate on finding the house where Mary's grandmother lived.

After about fifteen minutes, he arrived at the house on the outskirts of Manchester, and like Donald, he couldn't help but be impressed. It had never occurred to him that Bunty came from a wealthy family. She was a working woman, a schoolteacher. But someone who lived in a house like this wouldn't need to work. Yet there was Mary training to be a nurse. What she was doing was admirable in his eyes.

When he had settled into the guest room and dined with Mary and her grandmother, he and Mary went for a walk. It was a beautiful summer evening, and they could hear the crickets humming in the hedgerows. Various crops were peeking through

134

the furrows in the fields, their green shoots vibrant against the brown earth. It made Roddy think of Uist. The vegetables they grew there were meagre in comparison with this abundant crop, but he felt a longing to be in the fields again with his grandfather. It surprised him, as he rarely felt nostalgic for the island and his old life. He must be getting soft. Mary interrupted his thoughts.

'I expect you're wondering what happened today when we bumped into each other.'

'Yes. You were so upset I couldn't help wondering if your uncle had forbidden you to marry Donald.'

'No. It was nothing like that. My grandmother and Uncle Charles liked Donald and gave us their blessing.'

'I'm glad to hear it. My brother is a good man. May I ask then what upset you so much?'

'It was something my uncle told me about my mother. I know you're not fond of her and blame her for your father's death, so I don't expect you to be sympathetic. But I think you'll understand why I was so upset when I tell you what he said.'

Roddy felt his soft feelings leaving him at the mention of Bunty Hepworth. But he listened to Mary's story and found that he had some sympathy for Bunty.

'I didn't have time to hear what happened to my baby sister as my crying embarrassed my uncle and he asked me to move out of the café. That's when I bumped into you.'

'So, they locked your mother up in an asylum because she was having a baby. Then when the baby died, they wouldn't let her leave because she wouldn't stop telling people what had happened?'

'More or less. But, of course, it wasn't just for that reason. She was ill, as you know, on the day of your father's funeral. I remember being terrified when she began talking to Uncle Johnny even although he was in Canada.'

Roddy wondered what Uncle Johnny had to do with all this. He knew his uncle had befriended Bunty, but surely their relationship hadn't been more than that.

135

'It must have been awful for you, Mary. I'm so sorry. But how awful for your mother too, losing her baby and then have people wanting her to pretend it hadn't happened.'

'I know Uncle Charles and my grandma were doing it for what they thought were the right reasons, but to not acknowledge the birth of a child is monstrous. I don't even know if my sister had a proper burial.'

'So, what do you want to do?'

'I want to find out what happened to the child's body, but I also want to visit where my mother lived for that year. I hate to think of her being locked up in some awful asylum. You hear such terrible stories of these places.'

'How can I help?'

'I was wondering if you would come with me to the asylum once I find out where it is.'

'I'll do whatever you ask, Mary. When would you like to go?'

'You're being very kind to me, Roddy. Thank you.'

She put her hand on his, and his breath caught in his throat at her touch. He put his hand to his mouth and coughed to cover up his confusion. What was happening to him?

'I'd like to go tomorrow if you can spare the time. I know you'll be keen to get on with your travels and I only have another three days here.'

'Yes, that'll be fine, Mary.'

'When we get home, I plan to ask my grandma where they took my mother, so I hope you don't mind going to your room early so that I can question her.'

'No problem at all. I'm quite tired, anyway.'

They turned and made their way back to the house and the great yellow sun sinking into the horizon bathed them in its twilight glow. Roderick had an urge to take Mary's hand and wondered again what was happening to him.

CHAPTER FORTY-SEVEN

After Roddy had gone to bed, Mary sat with her grandmother in the small sitting room, where they used to spend time together when she was a child. How she had loved those times with her grandma. They gave her a feeling of security that she had never experienced with her mother. Her poor mother. What had made her the way she was? Had something awful happened to her that Mary didn't know about, or was it just a cruel act of nature that she suffered from mental illness? Next year she would get the chance to work in Glasgow Royal Mental Hospital, which catered for the insane. She hoped the experience would give her a greater understanding about mental ill health. After all, it was her experience in the women's ward that had helped her realise the truth about her mother.

Tonight, she was less relaxed as they sat listening to the BBC Symphony Orchestra on the wireless than she used to be as a child. But when the programme ended, the opportunity to chat presented itself.

'Well Mary, we've had a quiet night tonight. Quite like old times, wasn't it?'

Mary smiled, but her heart was beating fast at what she was about to say.

'Grandma, can I ask you something about Mummy?'

'About your mummy?'

'Yes. There's something I need to ask you.'

'Alright Mary. I'm listening, lass.'

'Where was she sent when she left the asylum in North Uist?'

'Oh Mary. Why do you want to know that? It's all so long ago. Sometimes it's best to let sleeping dogs lie.'

'I can't. I need to know what life was like for her in that asylum. I've heard such terrible stories.'

'You don't need to worry about that. She went to Cheadle Royal Hospital. It's a private hospital that caters for people with money, and the doctors there took a modern approach to dealing with mentally ill patients.'

She was relieved, but then asked what she really wanted to know the answer to.

'What happened to the baby my mother had when she was in there?'

'She didn't have a baby, Mary. It was her illness that made her tell you that story about having a baby.'

'I know the truth, Grandma. I asked Uncle Charles today, and he confirmed it was true. Please don't keep lying to me.'

Her grandmother rose slowly from her chair and walked over to the window. It was dark apart from the moon shining outside the window, but she continued to stare into the night.

'What made my mother the way she is, Grandma? Why does she suffer from mental illness?'

Without looking at her, Grace told her about her mother.

'I'm not sure how much you know about this, Mary, but I'll tell you the truth, although it causes me pain to do so. I'm ashamed of much that I'm about to reveal to you.'

She said nothing as she waited for her grandmother to continue. She didn't wish to cause her grandmother any anguish, but she needed to know everything.

'When I was just 18, I met and fell in love with James Adams. I made the mistake of trusting him, but when he found out I was pregnant, he ran off to Canada. We both came from poor families, so I didn't really blame him. Life was hard in those days. There were no unemployment payments or pensions. My father told me I would need to get rid of the baby or find a husband to support me, as he couldn't afford another mouth to feed. I was the oldest of seven children, you see, and my parents relied on me to work to help support the family.'

Grace was quiet for a while, still staring out of the window, and Mary wondered where her thoughts had gone to.

'I'm ashamed to say I decided to get rid of my baby, but I didn't have the money to pay for the woman who helped with such things. So, I asked James's brother, Frederick, to help. He had a rag and bone business and was doing okay with it. He was determined to make money so that he could escape from the rat-infested streets where we lived by the canal, but he was also a Methodist and believed in God. I thought he might help me for that reason. He helped me, but not in the way I thought, and that's why your mother lived.'

Her grandmother's voice changed as she related the conversation that had taken place between her and Frederick Adams.

" 'Our James has gone and left you up the duff, has he?'

'Yes, and I was wondering if you could find it in your heart to give me the money to pay Mrs Maloney to get rid of it.'

'God forgive you, woman, for suggesting such a thing to me. That baby is my flesh and blood, and I shall not let you get rid of it.'

'But I cannot support a child, Freddie. I shall have to throw myself in the canal if you don't help me.'

'Throw thyself in the canal? God forgive you again, woman. You are nothing but a rotten sinner, but I shall take pity on you. It's my Christian duty.'

'What do you mean?'

'I shall marry you and bring the child up as my own. No one need ever know the truth.' "

'And that's what he did. But he never let me forget it and he was cruel to your mother. She left home as soon as she could and married your father to get away from him.'

'But when mother and I stayed with you, I remember him playing with me and giving me sweets.'

'Oh yes, he could be kind. He was always kind to your Uncle Charles, his own child. But he was never kind to Bunty. No wonder she took a breakdown when Harry died, and she had to bring you home to live with us. She must have worried that he would be cruel to you, but he never was. His greatest cruelty was in using his influence to make the psychiatrist at Cheadle Royal Hospital keep her in after she had you. That's why you and she never bonded properly. Your poor mother had a terrible young life and I pray to God every day that she's happy now.'

Grace turned from the window, her face lined with tears that flowed unchecked.

'Please don't try to find the child, Mary.'

'But I need to know where she is, Grandma. Did you give her a proper burial? Is she buried in the cemetery beside Grandpa?'

Grace's face became confused.

'What exactly did your uncle tell you, Mary?'

'He told me mummy had a baby girl, but she died. He didn't have time to tell me what happened to her body as he had to hurry for his train and by that time we had bumped into Roddy.'

Grace walked over to the window again and looked out into the moonlit night.

'I take it from your silence that you and Uncle Charles didn't bury the child in our family plot.'

Grace turned to face her. How old and haggard her grandma looked. She had never noticed it before.

'No, we didn't. The hospital made the arrangements for her burial. I believe they have a small area where they bury babies who are stillborn.'

They were both silent for a long time, and then Grace spoke again.

'Please don't contact your mother, Mary. She has settled well in Canada, and it would do no good raising all these secrets from the past. Who knows how it might affect her?'

'I think you're right. I won't tell her what I know. Thank you for being so honest with me. It makes sense of why Mummy is the way she is.'

'I'm going to bed now, Mary. I hope you don't dwell too much on what I've told you. You have your whole life ahead of you with that young man, Donald. Look forward and make the best of the life to come. We can't change the past, no matter how much we may want to. I shall see you in the morning.'

She kissed her grandma's wrinkled cheek, full of remorse at how drawn and pale she was. She expected neither of them would get much sleep that night.

CHAPTER FORTY-EIGHT

Roddy was up early the next day, ready for the quest he and Mary would go on. A waft of fried bacon greeted him as he made his way downstairs to the dining room, and his stomach rumbled pleasantly in anticipation. He was happy. The day spread out before him, and the prospect of spending it with Mary felt good. He wasn't certain how they would get to the asylum, but he was sure she wouldn't want Stanley to drive them. Perhaps they could go on the Norton. In his mind's eye, he could almost feel her arms wrapped around his waist as they drove through the countryside. The only problem was girls normally rode in the sidecar, but he didn't have one of those. He walked boldly into the dining room, ready to wish everyone a good morning, but it was empty. While he waited, he gazed out of the window, enjoying the warm glow of the morning sunshine, and hummed along to the wireless playing softly in the background. He looked at his watch just as Betty came in.

'Good morning Mr Macdonald. I'm afraid Mrs Adams isn't feeling too good this morning, so she won't be down for breakfast. She asked me to tell you how sorry she was. Miss Mary is just checking on her and will join you shortly. But she said to start without her.'

'Oh, I'm sorry to hear Mrs Adams is poorly. I hope it's nothing serious.'

'There's bacon and scrambled eggs in the dishes on the sideboard. Please help yourself. I shall bring you some fresh toast and tea.'

Roddy helped himself but didn't enjoy it as much as he had expected. What if Mrs Adams was ill because Mary had asked her about the asylum? Perhaps they wouldn't be going anywhere today after all.

The door opened, and Mary walked in, looking rather washed-out. He got up and drew a chair out for her.

'Sit down Mary. Let me get you some bacon and eggs.'

'I'm not hungry, Roddy. I'll just have tea and toast.'

'Betty is just bringing some fresh. Tell me what's wrong.'

Mary's eyes glistened.

'I've upset my grandma, asking her about my mother and her time in the sanatorium. I feel so bad Roddy. I wish I'd never brought the matter up.'

'But you felt it was important to find out the truth. Do you still feel like that?'

'Yes, and no. I'm glad I asked my grandma, as what she told me made sense of the reason my mother is the way she is. I feel so sorry for her. Apparently, my grandpa was very cruel to her, and it was his fault my mother and I never bonded properly. He persuaded the chief psychiatrist, Mr Lamont, at Cheadle to keep her there after I was born and after she had the baby that died.'

'What about the baby? Do you still want to go to the asylum and find out what happened to it?'

'My grandma thinks I should let things be and concentrate on my future with Donald. I know she's right, but I can't help thinking if the child had lived, it would be the same age as your sister Heather.'

There was a pause as they both thought about Heather. Roddy felt bad, as he remembered how upset she had been when he was horrible to everyone at Maude's house. She was such a bonnie wee thing.

'Imagine what it would do to her if she suddenly found out Chrissie wasn't her mother.'

He went cold, as he remembered what it was like when Roderick and Chrissie told them they weren't Donald's parents.

'What's wrong Roddy. You look like you've seen a ghost.'

'I've not seen a ghost, Mary, but it makes me go cold when I think what it did to Donald and me when we found out Chrissie and Roderick weren't Donald's parents. We were never the same after that.'

'I'm sorry to raise such terrible memories for you, Roddy. I think it best if we don't pursue what happened to the child, don't you?'

143

'But didn't you want to see where they kept your mother?'

'Yes, but Grandma told me Cheadle Royal Hospital is a private hospital for people like my mother, so I don't feel so concerned now. My grandma's right. I need to think about Donald and our future together as husband and wife.'

He nodded and smiled. How lucky Donald was to have a woman such as Mary to love him. His spirits dipped as he'd been looking forward to spending the day with her, but it looked like it wasn't to be. Best if he just cleared out and went on his way.

'Look Mary, I think if we're not going to the asylum, I'll continue my travels. Do you mind?'

'No, of course not. It's probably for the best, as my grandma's not feeling great. But I've something to ask before you go.'

'Yes. What is it?'

'Could I ride with you a short way on your motorcycle? I so envy you the freedom to travel around the country the way you're doing.'

He grinned. There was nothing in the world he would rather do.

CHAPTER FORTY-NINE

Life felt good. He was engaged to be married to a wonderful girl, and he was going on a Hunger March with Jimmy. He hadn't gone on the march to London last year, as he was meeting Mary on one of her rare days off. It was more important to him, at that time, to see her. Not that it wasn't important now. Of course, it was. But when she asked him to go to Manchester, and he realised it coincided with the march, he had felt torn. So, the compromise was that he went to Manchester only for two days so that he would be back on time to go on the march.

When he reached the house and put his key in the lock, he could hear voices and wondered if Jimmy was having a meeting. He sometimes had party members round if there was something they needed to discuss. He knocked, intending only to let him and Annie know he was back, but when he opened the door, they called him in.

'Come in Donald. This is our daughter Rosemary. She arrived home yesterday.'

A girl about his own age sat at the kitchen table, looking quite at home. She had auburn wavy hair cut short to her chin and bright brown eyes which were looking at him with curiosity.

'Hello Donald,' she said, rising from the table and putting out her hand. 'I'm pleased to meet you. My Ma and Da have been telling me all about you.'

It surprised him how strong a grip she had, but somehow it reflected her personality. There was nothing shy about her and she was obviously comfortable meeting someone new. He was glad, as her confidence radiated to him and he shook her hand as enthusiastically as she had shaken his.

'I'm pleased to meet you too, Rosemary. Are you home for the march to Edinburgh?'

'No, I knew nothing about it, but I shall go along with you and my Da tomorrow. I've been away too long and am looking forward to meeting up with the Comrades in Scotland again.'

'May I ask where you've been?'

145

'Didn't Da tell you? I've been to Russia.'

He felt a quiver of unease. Russia? It was one thing to be supporting the hunger marchers, but he wasn't sure how he felt about someone who had been to Russia. Weren't they trying to promote revolution in Britain and elsewhere?

'You look a little anxious about that, Donald. You don't support the Fascists, do you?'

'No, of course, he doesn't,' said Jimmy. 'He wouldn't be coming on the march tomorrow if he did. Now get off your soapbox and let the boy get to bed.'

'I am quite tired. It's a long trip from Manchester. Good to meet you, Rosemary. See you tomorrow.'

The following morning, they were up and ready before sunrise. Jimmy had one of the new folding wheelchairs, so they took a taxi to George Square, where the march would begin. Hundreds of well-wishers thronged the square, and there was an air of excitement as the marchers set off. They were led by Harry McShane of the NUWM and leaders of the Communist Party and the ILP. The crowd cheered and clapped as they began marching, with bands playing and banners flying. It was a privilege for him to be marching with this unemployed army of men and women, all fighting for justice. It wasn't easy. The rain pelted down, and the authorities refused them proper accommodation. Many of the marchers suffered from blisters on their feet, but they prevailed. All along the route, people came out dropping coins they could ill afford into their collecting cans and wishing them well.

Rosemary was an energetic and interesting companion. She talked a little about her time in Russia, but he supposed she didn't want to say too much because of his reaction last night. She led the singing when they strode into Holyrood Palace, despite being directed in the opposite direction. He would never forget the sound made by the marchers' triumphant voices. They sang *The Internationale* in the very place where Rizzio and Mary Queen of Scots had made their own music. It was Rosemary who encouraged the marchers to bed down on Princes Street when the authorities refused them accommodation. And in the morning, she helped serve steaming hot tea from large dixie cans brought up from the field kitchen. Jimmy certainly had a daughter to be proud of. On the buses home, everyone agreed progress was made despite the Secretary of State for Scotland's refusal to meet them. They had shown solidarity against the establishment.

That night when they were sitting talking about what had happened, Rosemary asked Donald if he would write an article about it.

'You want to be a writer, don't you, Donald? This could be your big chance to get published. I know the editor of the Daily Worker so could show him your piece.'

Despite his time on the Gilmorehill Globe editorial team, he wasn't sure he was ready to be published. What if what he wrote was rubbish?

'I'll have a go Rosemary, but will you be honest when you read it? I've never contemplated writing an article for a newspaper. It's completely different from what I do on the Gilmorehill Globe.'

'Well, now's the time, Donald. You have a go and I'll let you know what I think.'

And so it was that his first piece of professional writing was for The Daily Worker.

CHAPTER FIFTY

After Roddy left, Mary spent the remaining three days of her holiday with her grandma, and put aside all thoughts of her baby sister. Stanley drove them out to a country pub for lunch one day and, on another, took them into Manchester to see a picture show. Mary would have liked to see King Kong, but Grace preferred something less dramatic. So they went to see Little Women starring Katharine Hepburn instead. These trips perked Grace up, and by the time she was ready to go home, her grandma was much brighter and happier. She was grateful for this, as the last thing she wanted was to upset her grandma.

On the train journey back to Glasgow, she thought a lot about Roddy. He'd been so easy to talk to and had been willing to help her in her quest to find out about her mother's baby. He was also exciting to be with. She wondered what Donald would think about her going on the motorcycle with him. Would he disapprove? But oh, it had been so deliciously thrilling. At first, she had clung onto him for dear life as the bike zoomed noisily out of the driveway and onto the road. She had never experienced such speed, and it felt like there was very little protection if they were to end up in a ditch. But gradually she had relaxed. He had yelled at her to move with him to keep the bike steady. When she did so, their bodies swayed together in perfect harmony as he manoeuvred the bike round the curves in the country roads. The feel of the sun on her back and the summer breeze rippling through her hair was so exquisite she could have ridden behind him forever. She was quite breathless when he drove her back home and her face flushed as she recalled the pleasure of having her arms around his waist.

Donald met her from the train, hugged her, and then kissed her lightly on the lips. She wished he would kiss her more ardently; the way he had during that first kiss, but she knew he would feel embarrassed kissing her in a public place like this. As they walked hand in hand to get the subway from Buchanan Street to Hillhead, he asked her how things had gone. Had she been able to find out anything helpful? She told him what Grace had told her.

'She was so upset, Donald, so I agreed I would not visit Cheadle Hospital or make any more inquiries about where they buried my sister. Sometimes it's best to leave things in the past, don't you agree? Roddy said you and he were never the same after you found out Chrissie and Roderick weren't your parents.'

'You saw Roddy?'

'Oh yes, he turned up in the station cafe the day you travelled home. Didn't he tell you?'

'I haven't seen him. He's still travelling. So how did you two get on?'

Mary smiled widely as she thought of Roddy and that exhilarating motorbike ride they had taken together.

'We got on great, Donald. Your brother is actually an extremely amiable person when you get to know him.'

She was about to go on and tell him about the motorbike ride when she noticed he looked a little disappointed, so she changed her mind.

'But he's not you, Donald. I would have much preferred to spend all my holidays with you.'

He smiled and squeezed her hand.

'So where will you be working when you start back tomorrow?'

'Surgical I think.'

'Rather you than me, Mary,' he grimaced, then continued. 'Now we're engaged, do you think we should think about setting a date for our marriage?'

'I think we should, but it can't be till after we finish our studies.'

'That's true, so I think we should become officially engaged.'

'You mean buy a ring and everything?'

'I do. On your next day off, you and I shall go to the Argyll Arcade and buy you a ring.'

'What's the Argyll Arcade?'

'It's a covered shopping arcade that links Buchanan Street and Argyle Street. It has milliners, dressmakers, toy shops and jeweller's shops that sell engagement rings. I only know as Roddy took me to Sloan's Bar there when I arrived in Glasgow. It's a beautiful place with a domed glass ceiling.'

'I can't wait for my next day off,' she cried, and throwing caution to the wind, she kissed Donald fully on the lips and was delighted when he ardently returned her kiss.

CHAPTER FIFTY-ONE

Roddy had been reluctant to leave Mary, but he knew she wanted to use the rest of her break to make up for upsetting her grandmother, and he didn't want to intrude. He'd enjoyed her company so much and had loved their ride together on his motorbike. She was a natural. As he made his way out of Manchester, he noticed an imposing Victorian building with a sign outside declaring it to be Cheadle Royal Hospital. Wasn't that the place Mary said they had taken her mother? On impulse, he stopped, parked up his bike and walked up towards the gates. On the stone wall at the side of the gate was a notice declaring that 'Visitors are admitted by appointment only'. Just then, a middle-aged man walked up the road. He nodded to Roddy, lit a cigarette, and stood beside him.

'Are you visiting someone?' he asked.

'No, I'm a solicitor and I'm trying to trace a relative for a client of mine.'

He found the lie came easily to his lips.

'You look too young to be a solicitor.'

'Well, I'm still in training. It takes several years to become qualified, you know.'

'You don't sound local. Where are you from?'

'I'm from Scotland.'

'Hmm. And who's this relative you're trying to find for your client?'

'Well, it's confidential.'

Their conversation was interrupted, when several other people joined them, obviously about to begin their shift.

'Hello Bert. Ready for another day in the nuthouse?' said a young woman.

'Now, now Nancy, it's not nice to talk about the patients like that.'

She laughed.

'Why not? They don't know any better the way them doctors dope them up with drugs.'

'Here's Sister coming. Better not let her hear you talking like that,' the man said.

The gates scraped open, and the waiting employees filed in, all except Bert, who finished his cigarette.

'Can I help you?' the Sister asked, looking Roddy up and down.

'I hope so. My name's Roddy Macdonald. I'm a solicitor and am making inquiries on behalf of a client and I wondered if I might speak to someone.'

'Regarding what?'

'Well, it's confidential, but it's about a woman who was brought here twelve years ago. I'm wondering if it would be possible to have access to her records.'

'All records are confidential. I'm afraid you would need to make an appointment.'

'Unfortunately, I'm leaving tomorrow. Would it be possible to see the person in charge now?'

'No, I'm sorry. He's at a conference for the next three days. Perhaps it would be better if you wrote in with your request.'

She turned on her heel and made her way back up to the house, leaving Roddy full of disappointment.

'Maybe I could help you,' said Bert, who had finished his cigarette and was stubbing it out underfoot.

'In what way? Do you have access to confidential records?'

'No need to be sniffy with me. Of course, I don't have access to confidential records, but I have an excellent memory,' he said, tapping the side of his forehead. 'And I've worked here for over twelve years.'

Roddy looked at the man, weighing up the pros and cons of telling him anything. Before he could reply, he heard the Sister calling, telling Bert to get inside, and shut the gate.

'If you want to talk about your client, I could meet you in the Dog and Duck tonight when I finish at 9 o'clock. It's just along the road. But you would need to make it worth my while. Porter's wages aren't much, you know, and I have a lot of mouths to feed.'

Roddy carried some money on him, but he wasn't sure how much the man would want. Also, he wasn't sure he could trust him. He could make up a story just to get his money.

'But how do I know you can help me?'

'You don't, but it sounds to me like you have no other option if you want to help your client.'

Bert made his way inside the grounds and the gate clanged shut behind him.

CHAPTER FIFTY-TWO

My Dear Mummy

I hope this letter finds you well and happy. I'm writing to let you know Donald and I are now engaged to be married. Grandma and Uncle Charles approve, and I sincerely hope you do too. Although he's not very rich, he bought me a beautiful diamond and sapphire engagement ring. I don't wear it on the wards in case it gets lost or damaged, but any time we go out I parade about like a peacock showing it off.

We haven't set a date for the wedding yet, as we need to finish our studies first. Is it possible you could make the journey home for it? If not, Donald and I will come out to visit you. He wants to find out more about his ancestors and I, of course, want to see you. It's a strange thing, but Donald has lost the shame he always felt about his grandmother being a native Canadian. It came about when he discovered that someone with the same surname as Lily was a war hero.

I'm so happy Mummy. Donald is a good man. He has a kind temperament, and I know I shall have a secure, safe life with him. His brother Roddy is also a good man but is more impulsive than Donald and sometimes gets himself into scrapes because of his hot-headedness. He ended up in hospital after a severe beating by his girlfriend's father and that was when I got to know him better. I wondered how he would feel about Donald and me getting together, but I'm happy to tell you he too has approved, as has Auntie Chrissie. I think they have forgiven you for the past, realising that it was your illness that made you act the way you did. So, all will be well if you decide to come to the wedding.

We have a lot of time to make up and have so much to talk about, Mummy, so I can't wait to see you again. Do take care of yourself and write back to me soon with your thoughts on my news.
With great affection,
Your loving daughter,
Mary

CHAPTER FIFTY-THREE

I looked out the window and almost fainted when I saw Roddy. What on earth was he doing here? He had written to tell me he was travelling the length and breadth of the British Isles and probably wouldn't be home during the summer. But here he was, looking handsome and healthy. Heather was out playing with her friends, father was out mending a fence and mother was making butter.

'Roddy,' I called, running out of the house. '*Ciamar a tha thu?* It's wonderful to see you. Come away in.'

'Hello *Mathair*,' he said, slipping easily back into the Gaelic. 'I'm great. Get the kettle on, will you? I'm parched.'

When he had had his tea and a scone, he settled down beside the fireplace, which was empty of peats at this time of year. My breath caught in my throat as I gazed at him; he looked so like Roderick.

'So, tell me all about your travels, son. Where did you get to and what's brought you up here? I thought you weren't coming this year. Granny and Grandad will be so happy to see you.'

I paused for breath, knowing I was talking too much. Happiness and anxiety made me do that. I still missed him so much and had a secret hope that he might come back and take over Mr Abernethy's practice in Lochmaddy once he qualified. But when he coughed, a sure sign that he was nervous about what he was about to say, my heart sank. Memories of that day in Maude's house still made me anxious. How I hated confrontation, especially between my two boys. Although Roddy had told me all was well, I couldn't help wondering if it was. What would make him come home?

'I want to talk to you about someone I met while I was travelling, *Mathair*. That's why I've come home even although I didn't plan to.'

'Someone you met. Is it someone I know?'

'No, but it's someone who knew Bunty when she was in the Sanatorium in Manchester.'

'Bunty?'

'Yes.'

I said nothing more. Best to let him say what he was about to say and then I could decide how I wanted to answer him, but my heart sank at the mention of Bunty's name. Was I never to be free of her presence haunting me?

'The man I met was called Bert, and he was a porter in the sanatorium where Bunty's brother took her after leaving Uist. As chance would have it, I was passing and stopped just when he was beginning his shift. I pretended to be a solicitor acting on behalf of my client, who was trying to trace a relative.'

I wanted to ask what he was doing down in Manchester and how he knew which Sanatorium they had taken Bunty to, but I kept quiet and let him continue.

'He asked me to meet him in one of the local pubs when he finished his shift, so that's what I did, and I found out something interesting.'

My stomach clenched. What had he found out that was so interesting it made him come home to question me about it? I broke my silence.

'What was that?'

'I found out that Bunty had a baby girl. Her uncle and her grandma told Mary the baby was stillborn, but Bert told me the baby lived.'

When I didn't respond, he continued.

'I also discovered they hadn't registered her birth there. Normal practice was to register children born in the asylum in the hospital's records, but it wasn't. According to Bert, Bunty's brother did a deal with the resident psychiatrist and took the baby for a private adoption. Apparently, it was all very cloak and dagger.'

'And did this Bert know anything about who Bunty's brother gave the baby to?'

'No. But he told me something else that I think will interest you.'

156

'What was that?'

I shivered. Was my secret about to be revealed? Had Roddy somehow discovered the truth?

'Well, he also told me he got talking to Bunty. She told him the baby's father had emigrated to Canada, and she felt guilty about the way she had treated him. She had only told him about the baby when it was too late for him to do anything about it. I think the baby's father was Uncle Johnny.'

Was that the big revelation?

'You don't look surprised, *Mathair*? Did you know?'

'No, of course, I didn't know. But if Bunty had a baby, then I would agree that the father was most likely my brother, as he was the only single man she was friendly with.'

'What do you think we should do with this information?'

'I don't know Roddy. What do you think we should do? By the sound of what this man Bert said, Bunty told Johnny she was having a child by him, so he already knows. It's not as if you've any information about the wee girl, is it?'

I held my breath, waiting for his reply.

'No, I don't, but originally, when Mary found out Bunty had a little girl, she was all set on finding out where they had buried her, but her grandma persuaded her not to. But if she knew the child had lived, she would want to know what happened to her. So, I'm going to find out for her.'

'Why would you want to do that?'

He looked at me, and I wondered if my words had been too curt. I could see him struggling with the question.

'Sometimes dogs are best left sleeping, Roddy.'

'I suppose you're right. The girl would be the same age as our Heather now. Imagine how Heather would feel if she suddenly found out you weren't her mother.'

'Not her mother. Don't be ridiculous Roddy. Of course, I'm her mother.'

'Don't get all hot and bothered, *Mathair*. I'm not saying you're not her mother, but it wouldn't be the first time you pretended to be someone's mother.'

'Oh Roddy, let's not go back over that old ground. That's all in the past. You know why your father and I pretended to be Donald's parents. I'm going out for a walk. I can't be doing with this anymore.'

By the time I grabbed my coat, I was shaking. I had handled that badly and prayed to God that I hadn't given the game away by protesting too much.

CHAPTER FIFTY-FOUR

He looked in amazement at his mother. What on earth was going on with her, losing her temper like that? He'd only mentioned that Bunty's baby would be the same age as Heather now, and it seemed to set her off. But why? Did she know something about Bunty's baby that she wasn't letting on? He knew he shouldn't have said what he did about her telling lies before about Donald, but he couldn't help it. Sometimes she just rubbed him up the wrong way, but it was unforgivable to bring it up again so soon after his outburst at Maude's house. He would need to keep better control of his tongue. As Maude had said, a prerequisite for being a lawyer was to remain calm and in control. But in the argument with his mother, they hadn't discussed the situation of Johnny being a father to Bunty's baby.

His thoughts went back to his mother's question about why he wanted to find Mary's sister. Why did he want to do it? Why didn't he just tell Mary what he now knew? To his astonishment, he realised it was because he wanted to please her. He wanted to do something big that would impress her, that would make a difference to her life. But why? She was Donald's fiancé. They were engaged to be married, but he was behaving as if it was he who was marrying her, as if he were her lover. Was he in love with Mary? That day when she rode on the back of his motorbike came into his mind and he realised it had been one of the most wonderful experiences of his life. He hadn't felt so happy in a long time. But it was wrong. She belonged to his brother and could never be his. He would need to think about this and keep his distance. He didn't want to hurt them, but he kept seeing Mary's face and the way her eyes lit up when she saw him. Perhaps she had feelings for him, too.

Not long after his mother had slammed out the door, his grandparents came in. As expected, they welcomed him with open arms.

'Och Roddy, it's been such a long time since we've seen you. You're getting too big for your boots now that you're a graduate of that University of Glasgow,' said his grandad.

'Don't be daft *Seanair*, I'll always remember where I've come from. Have you got some chores I could help you with while I'm here? I might as well make myself useful.'

There was nothing he liked more than being out with his grandad.

'Well, some crops are ready for pulling, so you can help me with that.'

'And I'll bake some fresh scones for you. Where's your *mathair*?'

'I'm not sure. She went in a mood with me about something and went for a walk.'

'You two. I don't know what you have to argue about. You've only just come home.'

'I mentioned something I'd found out about Bunty Hepworth.'

His granny's body stiffened, and her smile turned to a frown.

'What did you find out about that woman? It's a pity our Donald has fallen for her daughter.'

'Mary's a lovely girl, *Seanmhair*. Donald's lucky to have her.'

His grandmother raised her eyebrows but said nothing.

'I found out Bunty had a baby girl when she was in the asylum in Manchester but that her brother arranged a private adoption, so they didn't register the baby there.'

'And what's that to do with you?'

'Well, nothing really. It's just that Mary's uncle told her Bunty's baby had died.'

As he spoke the words, Charles's face came into his mind again and he remembered how he knew him. He was the man who had told them all the lies about his family and has shopped Jimmy to the police. It was his fault Jimmy ended up in the hospital and now needed a wheelchair. All his former hatred of Bunty Hepworth resurfaced. He had felt sorry for her when Mary told him about her mother. But knowing what he now knew about Charles Adams

160

made him think that badness just ran in the family. Donald was welcome to Mary. He wanted nothing else to do with her and certainly wouldn't be going looking for her sister.

'What's wrong Roddy? You look like you could murder someone.'

'I could *Seanair*, I could. I've just remembered something, and it's made me angry. But let's not talk about it. I'd rather go outside with you. I'll be going back to Glasgow tomorrow, so you need to make the most of me being here.'

'Aye Laddie, hard work is the best answer for an angry mind.'

CHAPTER FIFTY-FIVE

On his journey back from North Uist, Roddy realised his life was about to change completely. Maude had helped him get an apprenticeship with the firm where she had served hers, and he was due to start in October. He was looking forward to it and hoped his dream of becoming a successful criminal lawyer would come true. But what he'd realised at the croft was worrying him. He couldn't believe he had feelings for Mary Hepworth. How could that have happened? Because of her mother, he had disliked her so much. But that had all changed after Mr Dunlop beat him up. It was Mary's face he had woken up to in the hospital. He had thought she was an angel, and he recognised he still did despite his rage when he realised it was her uncle who had shopped Jimmy to the police.

His head was telling him to have nothing more to do with that toxic family, but his heart was saying something else. What was he going to do about it? It was unthinkable that he would try to win Mary away from Donald. He was his brother. It would be the lowest form of betrayal. Yet he hated the thought of his brother marrying into that family. Perhaps he would be doing him a favour. Wait until he told Donald what he knew. He was sure to call off his engagement to Mary. Donald wouldn't want to marry the niece of a man like Charles Hepworth. But what about Mary? What would she do when she found out her uncle had lied to her and that her sister was alive somewhere? She would be lost without Donald when she received such devastating news. As he went over all this in his mind, he realised he wouldn't do any of the things he was thinking. He loved his brother and Mary and would hate to hurt them. He would just need to stay out of their way as much as possible.

But it wasn't working. It was almost a year since he had found out his true feelings, and they were still there. No matter how he tried to distract himself, he couldn't stop thinking of her. It was becoming more and more difficult to make excuses to Donald for not meeting up with him and Mary. His brother looked so hurt when he kept turning him down because of work or his newfound interest in Scottish politics. But better that than stealing his girlfriend. Perhaps he was being rather sure of himself, though. Mary probably wouldn't give him the time of day. But he wouldn't take the chance. He decided it was time to leave the flat he shared with Donald and move into a place of his own. That way, it would be easier to avoid them.

CHAPTER FIFTY-SIX

When Roddy returned from his travels, something was different about him. Donald couldn't quite put his finger on what it was, but there was definitely a cooling off. While he knew things would be different, he hadn't expected Roddy to be so busy that he could no longer make time to meet with him and Mary. There always seemed to be some excuse. He was working late, or meeting up with work colleagues, it seemed. His newfound involvement in Scottish Nationalism, which came after he lost faith in the Labour Party, was taking up a lot of his time and energy, too. When he told him he was moving out, things had been different between them for almost a year.

'I'm moving out Donald. I hope you don't mind. I feel now that I'm no longer a student, it would be best for me to have my own place. You can get someone to share with you if you can't afford the rent. I know Jimmy and Annie won't mind.'

'Is that the only reason you're moving out, Roddy? You've been different with me this past year. It's like there's something I've done that you're not telling me about. Is it because you've become involved with the Scottish National Party? Are you unhappy with me being involved with Jimmy and Rosemary and writing for the Daily Worker?'

Roddy swept his hand through his hair, and it reminded Donald of Roderick. He used to do that when he was agitated.

'No, it's nothing to do with that. I'm happy you've found something you feel passionate about. But you're right. I have cut you and Mary out of my life, but it's not because you've done anything wrong.'

'What is it then?'

'I found out information about Bunty's baby and about Mary's uncle and decided it was for the best not to share it with you.'

Donald's stomach clenched. What could it be? Was it something that would affect his relationship with Mary? He felt things between them were already not quite right. They were becoming boring, like an old married couple with their routines. Without Roddy to jildy him along, they never went dancing and rarely even went to the pictures now. Even though he wanted to get closer to her, he was uncertain he could keep his desires in check, so avoided becoming overly affectionate. He sensed Mary wanted more, but she said nothing. It was like an elephant in the room; this desire that they couldn't express.

So, he tried to express it in another way. Each time he met her, he gave her a poem written on special quality bond paper, which he folded and sealed with wax. The first time he'd given her one, she had cried and kissed him.

'Oh Donald, that's the most romantic gesture anyone could make. Thank you, thank you, my darling. And what a wonderful poet you are. I'm sure you'll be famous one day.'

But it, too, had become just another one of their routines after a while.

'Tell me now, Roddy. You can't leave without letting me know what's been bothering you.'

CHAPTER FIFTY-SEVEN

Roddy looked at Donald. It would be easy to say it was because he had become interested in Scottish Nationalism. His original ambition to be a politician was back on his agenda again. A partner in the firm he worked for was a member of the recently formed Scottish National Party and he'd invited him along to some meetings. He had found it so interesting and felt this party might suit him better than the Labour Party, who had let their members down so disgracefully. Wasn't he always going on about Land Reform and the plight of crofters? Scotland, having its own government, could put paid to the old land ownership rules and change things for the better. But it wasn't straightforward. There were different views in the Party about the best way forward. Some wanted complete independence, others a Scottish Assembly within the UK. He hadn't made his mind up yet what he considered would work best.

But as he gazed at his brother's troubled face, he knew it was time to tell him the truth. Not the whole truth, of course. He would leave his feelings for Mary out of what he was about to tell him. So, he took a breath and then began.

'When I was down in Manchester, I passed the Cheadle Royal Hospital, which is where they took Bunty when she left North Uist. I got talking to a man who worked there years ago, and I asked him if he remembered Bunty and he told me he did. Everyone had made out she was very ill, but he thought she wasn't as bad as they said.'

'That would tie in with what Mary thinks.'

'Yes, but the significant revelation is that Bunty had a baby, but it didn't die as her Uncle Charles told her. '

'What? Are you sure? Can you trust what this man told you?

'He didn't have any reason to lie, Donald.

'That's scandalous. Just wait till I tell Mary?'

'Donald, I don't think you should tell her. What good would it do after all these years? Besides, it looks like Uncle Johnny was the baby's father.'

'Mary wondered about that, too. What's making you think that?'

'Bert told me that Bunty and he chatted. She told him she had treated the baby's father badly, but there was nothing she could do about it as he now lived in Canada. When I put it to Mother, she didn't seem the least bit surprised. So far as she knew, Johnny was the only man Bunty had been friendly with, so if she'd had a baby, then he was most likely the father.'

'You told Chrissie, but not me. Why?'

'I don't know. I thought maybe she would know something, but she didn't.'

'Well, I'm glad you've told me now. But you'll have to leave it up to me whether to tell Mary. She's going to be my wife, and it's not good for married couples to have secrets.'

'There's something else, Donald, and I'm not sure how you'll take it.'

Donald looked at him, clearly wondering what bombshell he was going to drop. But from the look on his face, what he told him was the last thing he expected.

'Mary's Uncle Charles is not to be trusted. I thought I knew him when I met him that time with Mary at Manchester station, but it only came back to me recently. Do you remember I told you about the agent provocateur who shopped Jimmy to the mounted police?'

Donald nodded.

'I do indeed. It was because of that man that Jimmy ended up in a wheelchair and why I've become more involved in politics. But what did he have to do with Mary's uncle?'

'Well, I'm almost a hundred percent sure that the man was Charles Adams.'

'My God, Roddy. That's a serious allegation. Are you absolutely sure it was him?'

167

'No, I can't be a hundred percent sure, but I think it was.'

'How can I marry Mary, knowing what her uncle has done? It would be a complete betrayal of Jimmy after all he's done for me.'

'That was partly why I didn't tell you, Donald. I know how fond you are of Jimmy, but you can't let Charles Adams split you and Mary up. You're meant for each other.'

The words were out of his mouth before he could stop them. This could have been his opportunity to stop Donald from marrying Mary, but he couldn't do it. His brother would be lost without her.

'How will I ever be able to look that man in the eye again? He'll be giving Mary away when we get married, but I shall find it hard to be civil to him after what you've told me.'

'Have you set a date for the wedding yet?'

'Yes. It'll be next summer after I've graduated, and Mary has finished her studies.'

'I take it you still want me to be your Best Man?'

'Of course. Who else would I ask?'

CHAPTER FIFTY-EIGHT

It didn't surprise Mary as much as he had expected when he told her about Roddy moving out.

'Well, he's working and moving in different circles now. We've hardly seen him this last year, have we?'

What he didn't tell her was that her sister was still alive and that her Uncle Charles was a lying swine. Part of him wanted to tell her, but what good would it do? She would only spend too much time thinking about it and trying to find the child. He thought it would be unhealthy for her. She had a fear of inheriting her mother's mental health issues and he felt that brooding about her sister could lead to the very thing she dreaded. It would be better if she didn't know.

They were in his room, and he reflected on how good it was to have his own place where he could invite Mary. It was the main reason he didn't take another student in to stay with him. He preferred to pay the extra rent and have somewhere to take Mary. He'd initially been a little anxious about inviting her to his room, but she had been eager to visit him. Perhaps she was hoping they would become more intimate. Although they kissed more often than they did outside, he was always on guard against his feelings getting the better of him.

Without giving the game away, he tried to find out a bit more about her uncle. On the pretext of finding out if he could get away for the wedding, he asked her what Charles did for a living.

'He never said what he worked at when I met him.'

'No, he was too busy pumping you for information about how much money you had,' she smiled. 'He's only told me he works for the government. Maybe he works for MI5 and is a spy, so we better give him plenty of notice so that he can get time off.'

Despite Mary's joke about the ridiculousness of Charles being a spy, if he was the person Roddy had seen in London, then he was. How would Mary feel if she knew Charles had lied to her and that his involvement in the hunger march to London had led to

Jimmy being injured? He was sure she wouldn't want him to give her away. For a moment, he considered telling Mary the truth just for the satisfaction of not having to see that man again, but then common sense prevailed, and he kept silent.

'Well, we better decide where we're having it. I suppose it should really be in Manchester, as that's where you come from, Mary.'

Last year, they had agreed to have a summer wedding when they would both have finished their studies, but they hadn't decided where they would hold the wedding.

'Yes, but I don't have as large a family as you do, so maybe we should hold it in Glasgow. It will be easier for both our families to make the journey.'

'I don't think my granddad will come. He never leaves the island now.'

'Do you want to get married in Uist? Lochmaddy Church would be a lovely venue and then we could go to the Lochmaddy Hotel for a meal afterwards.'

'I can't believe you feel nostalgic about Lochmaddy.'

'It wasn't all bad, Donald. It was where I met you, after all.'

'I love you, Mary Hepworth, and if you want to get married in Lochmaddy, then so be it. Perhaps it would be good to lay the ghosts of the past to rest.'

She nodded, and he kissed her, happy they had settled on where they would hold the wedding.

1935

MARY'S QUEST

CHAPTER FIFTY-NINE

Sir Arthur visited Glasgow a few months before Donald's graduation and invited him to dine with him at his club. It impressed Roddy when Donald told him where they were meeting.

'Can't you wangle me an invitation, Donald? I hear all sorts of influential people are members of that club.'

'It would be awkward Roddy and I would have thought with you being a Scottish Nationalist, you wouldn't want to associate with the landowning classes.'

'I would put up with it, if it would help me meet people who matter. Sometimes, who you know is worth more than what you know. Besides, you're almost a Communist, so I'm surprised you're happy to go along.'

Donald was anything but happy to be going along and wished it was Roddy who was meeting Sir Arthur. He hated dressing up in smart suits, but he knew he couldn't go to meet Sir Arthur dressed in the casual clothes he preferred. When he arrived, he rang the bell, a polished brass pull type that rang discretely inside. A young man, dressed like a butler, opened the door. Only when he told him who he was meeting did he let him in. His feet sank into the thick piled carpet as he walked along a dark corridor to the dining room. With a flourish, the young man opened the door and Donald walked into a smoke-filled room full of middle-aged men enjoying hearty meals. Trying not to bite his nails, he walked behind the young man who escorted him to where Sir Arthur was sitting.

'Donald, my dear chap. It's lovely to see you. My, you've filled out and grown somewhat since I last saw you.'

'I would hope so, Sir Arthur. I was only 12 and I'm now 21.'

'And you've gained a sense of humour. Sit down. What would you like to drink?'

'I'll have a Coca-Cola, please.'

'I'm not sure we have that, sir,' said the young man who had brought him in.

'I'll just have some water then, thank you.'

'What's wrong with some sherry or a glass of wine, Donald? Are you part of the temperance movement like your ... eh, Roderick?'

He knew he had been going to say his father, but his father was a drinker, unlike Roderick. He felt sad when he thought about Roderick. Chrissie had told him he could choose who he believed was his grandfather, as there was no proof either way. But although he would prefer to think it was Roderick, he knew it wasn't.

'I much admired my grandfather, Sir Arthur, but I'm not against alcohol. It's just that it doesn't agree with me, so I don't take it. It's because of my Cree blood, I expect.'

Sir Arthur spluttered on his wine but said nothing. They chatted about this and that and then he put to him the question Donald was sure he was going to ask him.

'So, what are your plans? Do you see yourself returning to North Uist as the Factor? I would love it if you would and I'm sure your father would have loved it too.'

Donald smiled to himself at Sir Arthur's attempt to manipulate his feelings with a mention of his father.

'I'm afraid I could never be the Factor, Sir Arthur. I just don't have the temperament for it. I hate fishing and hunting, so I would be bad for business.'

When they had finished their lunch, they made their way through to the lounge to have coffee. Sir Arthur made a big show of introducing him to several people and, to Donald's surprise, one of them was Mary's Uncle Charles.

'Donald, what a surprise? It's a pleasure to see you again.'

'Oh, you two already know each other, then?'

Donald got the distinct impression the two men had arranged this meeting and were feigning surprise. What were they up to? They must think him an idiot.

'Hello Charles,' he said, almost choking on the words as he remembered Jimmy. 'Mary didn't say you were coming to Glasgow.'

173

'No. It was a last-minute thing, so I didn't have time to let her know. How is my niece?'

'She's well and looking forward to our wedding. You know we're having it in Uist. We felt since that's where we met, it would be a good place to have it.'

'Hmm. I would have thought with what happened with my sister, that you might want to have it anywhere but there. But it's your decision.'

'Yes, it is.'

Donald felt his hackles rising. After what Roddy had told him, he didn't like this man, and again wondered what he and Sir Arthur were up to. It soon became clear.

'I'm glad I've bumped into you. I have a proposition to put to you.'

'I'll leave you to it, Charles. Goodbye Donald. It was good to catch up with you. I'm only sorry you don't see your future as the Factor on North Uist, but I suppose it leaves the way open for you to take up a completely different career.'

He looked at Charles knowingly.

'Let's order some tea and I'll tell you what I want to talk to you about.'

CHAPTER FIFTY-EIGHT

He left the club, totally offended that Charles thought he could betray his friends like that. What a horrible man he was. He met Mary that night when she finished her shift, and they went back to his room. She was eager to hear what the club was like and what he had eaten, but she soon got the message that he wasn't interested in talking about that.

'You'll never guess who was in the club and just happened to bump into Sir Arthur.'

'Who?'

'Your Uncle Charles.'

'Uncle Charles? He never told me he was coming up to Glasgow.'

'Well, he wouldn't, would he? He's good at keeping you in the dark. His brief visit was hush, hush.'

'Donald, what's got into you? I thought you found him pleasant when you met him. He clearly liked you or he wouldn't have agreed we could be married.'

'I think it suited his purpose to have me marry into the family.'

'What do you mean? What's he done that's upset you so much?'

'He offered me a job.'

'A job? Well, that's good isn't it? You'll need to look for work when you graduate. I know you want to be a writer, but you need to pay the bills and look after me if I need to give up my job because of this marriage bar that the trade unions are supporting. Only until you become famous, of course.'

'Hilarious, Mary.'

'I'm sorry. So, what job did he offer you?'

'Spying.'

'Spying?'

'It turns out he's a member of MI5 and he wants to recruit me. He attempted to persuade me by saying I could pursue my writing, as I would get an income from them for transmitting information.'

175

'Oh, my goodness. I knew he worked with the government, but I thought he was just a civil servant. And would it be such a bad thing, Donald, to take a job in MI5? I believe that department is important for the safety and security of our country. They were very successful during the war at thwarting German spies.'

'You really think I should consider it?'

'Why not? You will need a job, all joking aside, so it would let you concentrate on your writing, which you really want to do.'

He was quiet. He would need to work, but surely not at the expense of betraying his friends.

'You don't know what he's asked me to do, Mary, and if you knew what I know about him, you wouldn't want me to work with him.'

'What's the terrible thing he's asked you to do?'

Mary's face was serious. He wished he could take back his words. What if she asked him what he knew about her uncle?

''His exact words were, *You're in an excellent position to find out more about the Commies because you live with Mr and Mrs Thompson. And you've been involved in some of the Hunger Marches so no one would suspect you of being one of us.'*

'It's mean of him asking you to spy on your friends, but couldn't we move away from Glasgow, and you could do some other work with MI5?'

'But it's the Communists they're interested in. They're worried about them sending people to spy on us.'

'But you're not a Commie. I don't see why you object so much.'

'It's not just the Communists they want to infiltrate, it's working-class people, too. They link the two and I can't condone that. I've seen people suffering because of the depression, but it doesn't make them all communists or revolutionaries.'

'I feel there's more that you're not telling me, Donald. Please don't keep secrets from me. It only makes matters worse.'

He hesitated, then decided she was right. He would tell her the truth and hope she would forgive him for not telling her sooner.

176

'Roddy saw your uncle in London when he went on the Hunger March in 1932. He was an agent provocateur and infiltrated their group. It was he who shopped Jimmy to the police and how he ended up in a wheelchair.'

'I can't believe my uncle would do such a despicable thing. Is Roddy sure?'

'Almost a hundred percent. He was there. He even felt sorry for him because of the story he told. But that's not the worst thing, my darling. He also lied to you.'

'Lied to me?'

'Yes. He told you your mother's baby was stillborn, but in fact she lived.'

'How do you know he lied? Why would he lie?'

Her voice was becoming shrill, and he wondered if he was doing the right thing by telling her. Perhaps his original decision had been the right one, but it was too late to stop now.

'Roddy spoke to someone at the sanatorium where your mother stayed. Apparently he was friendly with a Dr Lamont, the head psychiatrist there. He and Charles came to an arrangement not to register the child's birth there so that Charles could take the baby for a private adoption.'

'Dr Lamont? I wonder if he's the same doctor that I'm working with in the Royal. I shall ask him when I go to work tomorrow.'

Donald recalled this doctor's name coming up when Mary told him she'd started her final placement at the Glasgow Royal Mental Hospital. When he'd asked her if it was a good place to work, she had screwed her face up.

'Not really, Donald. It gives me the creeps. I always feel a little anxious when I'm going in. There are two sections to the hospital: one for people with money and one for the destitute. They lock doors on some wards to prevent patients from getting out. It's full of noise and screaming and people walking around looking blank. There's this Dr Lamont, and he likes to experiment with the patients. I'm not saying he's doing it for terrible reasons, but the effect of some things on the patients is horrendous.'

177

Mary's voice broke into his thoughts.

'Why would Uncle Charles lie about such a thing, Donald?'

Her face crumpled, and he took her in his arms.

'I suppose to stop you from trying to find the child and to protect the person who adopted her.'

She stayed in his arms for a few minutes and then pulled herself away. Her eyes were bright with tears, but they glinted with anger, too.

'How long have you known about this, Donald? It's been nearly two years since Roddy was in Manchester. Have you known all this time?'

CHAPTER FIFTY-NINE

Mary was enraged when Donald confessed he had known, but only for a year.

'Roddy only told me when he moved out of our flat last year.'

'You've known for a year! You and Roddy are a pair of liars. He went to Cheadle Hospital without my knowledge and then, when he found out what I wanted to know, he didn't tell me. But worse than that, you, my fiancée, didn't tell me either.'

'We were trying to protect you. Was that so wrong?'

'Yes, of course it was wrong. Didn't you think it was wrong when you found out Chrissie and Roderick had lied to you about your parentage?'

'No, I didn't. I wished I'd never found out the truth. It spoiled everything.'

She could see Donald was getting upset, but she didn't care. She was upset, too.

'Well, that was no reason not to tell me what you had found out, especially when you knew how upset I was when I realised my mother had been telling the truth about the baby. It wasn't your place to decide if I should know.'

'I'm sorry, Mary. It was for the best of reasons that I decided not to tell you. Don't you see? I didn't want you to brood.'

'To brood? What, were you worried I would end up like my mother in a lunatic asylum? How dare you Donald? I'm leaving now. I can't bear to look at you. And you can take this ring back too.'

She took the diamond and sapphire ring he had given her and threw it at him.

'Our engagement obviously means nothing to you.'

As she walked back to the nurses' home, she was distraught. She couldn't get out of her mind that they had taken her mother's little girl away and given her to someone else. Well, she was going to find out who had her sister and get her back and she would start off by asking Dr Lamont. Could he be the same doctor that Charles

179

had dealt with? What a lucky coincidence if he was. Perhaps he would even know who Charles had given the child to.

Although she slept badly, she rose early and went to work, determined to tackle the doctor, and find out what he knew. However, Sister asked her to help an orderly with a patient who was having a psychotic episode. The woman was screaming and begging someone they couldn't see to bring her baby back. As Mary and the orderly tried to calm her, she thought of her mother again that day at Roderick's funeral talking to Uncle Johnny. She recognised now that her mother had been having a psychotic episode just like this poor woman. But was the woman having one because someone really had taken her baby just like her uncle had taken her mother's baby? How difficult it was for the mentally ill. Doctors and nurses just assumed they were having a psychotic episode when they began hallucinating or talking to themselves. But what if they were speaking the truth, but no one believed them?

She felt her head spin and the next thing she knew; she was waking up in Sister's office.

'What happened, Sister?'

'You fainted, my girl. Are you finding working here a bit too much? Many of the trainees do.'

Mary wondered what to say. Should she tell the truth or try to cover up? She told the truth.

'My mother had mental health problems, Sister, and seeing that woman today reminded me of her. I'm sorry to have let you down.'

'Your placement is almost finished anyway, Mary, so I think it best if you take sick leave. That will tide you over until you finish up and get your qualification. Then I believe you plan to marry your sweetheart.'

Mary felt the tears starting again. Was she going to marry Donald after what he'd done? She wasn't sure anymore.

'Thank you, Sister. May I ask you something?'

'Yes, of course.'

180

'Do you know if Dr Lamont ever worked at Cheadle Royal Hospital near Manchester? That was where my mother went when she became ill.'

'I'm not too sure. He was here when I arrived, and I know little about him. May I ask why you want to know?'

'I wanted to ask if he remembered my mother.'

'I see. What's bothering you, Nurse Hepworth? I can see something has disturbed you. Has something happened to your mother?'

Mary found herself in floods of tears. She was making a complete fool of herself in front of Sister, so was bound to get a bad mark on her record for this placement. But she didn't care anymore. All she wanted to do was find her sister.

'Is there someone I can contact for you? You seem very distressed.'

'No. I shall be okay, Sister. Thank you for your kindness.'

Her world was empty. She had no one. Everyone just lied to her. But she would show them. She didn't need any of them. She would find out the truth on her own.

CHAPTER SIXTY

Donald was in his room writing when he heard a knock at the door and Rosemary going to open it. She then knocked on his door.

'Donald, there's a young woman to see you.'

His heart leapt. Was it Mary? He went to the door and saw Cynthia, and his hope turned to fear. Why was Cynthia here? Had something happened to Mary?

'Donald, Sister MacFarlane has asked me to come for you. Mary has locked herself in her room and won't come out. She was dreadfully upset when she came back from the Royal today.'

'Right, I'll just get my coat.'

Rosemary hovered about and asked him if he would like her to go along, but he said he thought it best if he saw Mary on her own.

He and Cynthia hurried along White Street, crossed over Byres Road and into Church Street. It wasn't a long walk, but Donald felt it was miles. They were quite out of breath by the time they arrived at the nurses' home. Cynthia let herself in with her key and took Donald past the night duty porters to the Sister Tutor's room.

'Ah, there you are, Mr Donaldson. Thank you for coming. You can go now, Nurse Walters.'

Cynthia left the room, and Sister MacFarlane continued. 'Your fiancé is very distressed and is refusing to come out of her room. Do you know what's wrong with her?'

'We had an argument, and she gave me back my ring. She was upset then, but I didn't realise it would affect her like this.'

'Well, come with me. I hope you can talk some sense into her. We can't have nurses breaking down and unable to do their shifts.'

Was Mary having a breakdown? It was the very thing he'd worried about, and the main reason he hadn't told her what Roddy had found out. When they reached Mary's room, Sister Tutor rapped on the door.

'Mary, your fiancé is here to see you. Please open the door. I shall be in my room if you need me.'

When Sister had left, Donald knocked gently.

'It's me, Mary. It's Donald. Please open the door, my darling, and tell me what's wrong.'

There was no answer and no sound of her door being opened for what seemed an age, and then he heard the scrape of a chair and footsteps. The door opened slowly and there she stood, looking at him with dull eyes. Her hair was in disarray, tears stained her cheeks, and her eyes were bloodshot from crying.

'Mary, sweetheart, what's happened? May I come in?'

She didn't answer, just turned away and walked back into her room, leaving the door open behind her. Used handkerchiefs littered the small dressing table where she sat. He kneeled in front of her and took her hands.

'I'm sorry for upsetting you, Mary. Please tell me how I can make it better.'

She began to cry again.

'You can't make it better, Donald. I'm my mother's daughter. I have a mental defect. You knew I wouldn't be able to handle the truth.'

'You've had a shock, Mary, that's all. Anyone would be upset. It doesn't mean there's anything wrong with you.'

'Why can't I stop crying then? Sister must think there's something seriously wrong with me to allow you, a man, to come visit me.'

Donald smiled inwardly. Was her mood lifting a little? He hoped so.

'I fainted at work and had to be sent home early and now Sister Tutor tells me I'm to go on sick leave until the course is finished.'

'I think that's a good idea. You've been overworking. Go home and spend some time with your Grandma. It will do you the world of good.'

'But she lied to me, Donald. How can I trust her anymore? I feel there's no one in the world I can trust anymore, not even you.'

183

'Oh Mary, you can trust me. Please tell me how I can help you and I shall do it. You're my world. I was only trying to protect you, but I can see I was wrong to do that. But I promise you I shall never, ever lie to you or refrain from telling you the truth as long as I live.'

Tears were trickling from his eyes now, and she put her fingers out to wipe them away.

'Help me find my sister, Donald. That's the only thing that will make me feel better.'

CHAPTER SIXTY-ONE

It surprised Roddy when he received a telephone call from Donald at the office, asking him to come round when he finished work as a matter of urgency. When he arrived, the last person he expected to see sitting at Jimmy's kitchen table was Mary, and a pale and bedraggled Mary at that. A wave of tenderness swept over him, and he rushed over to sit beside her. Taking her hands in his, he asked her gently what was wrong. Before she could answer, Donald came into the room, carrying a small travel bag. He looked pale too, but he was all business.

'Hello Roddy. Thank you for coming over. Would you be able to take Mary down to Helensburgh this evening on the Norton?'

'To Helensburgh?'

'Yes, to Aunt Morag's hotel. Mary needs a break and doesn't want to go home to Manchester. I've telephoned Morag, and she has a room available.'

'Yes, I'll be happy to take you, Mary. But why? What's happened?'

Mary told him all that had happened. He felt annoyed at Donald for telling her everything. He knew she was a sensitive girl and must have known it would upset her. But he supposed secrets between couples were wrong.

'It was wrong of you and Donald to keep what you found out from me, Roddy, but Donald has now agreed to find out all he can about my sister.'

'And how do you propose to do that, Donald?'

He couldn't keep the sarcasm out of his voice. It peeved him that Donald was to be the one to help Mary find her sister. Hadn't he been the one to find out the truth?

'I shall speak to Charles if he's still here and if not, I shall go to London if necessary. He's the key to this. If the man you spoke to is to be believed, then he did something underhand by not having the baby registered at the hospital.'

'But he's not going to just own up to that Donald. He'll say the man was lying.'

185

'There's also a Doctor Lamont working at the Royal Hospital,' said Mary eagerly. 'If he's the same man who did a deal with Uncle Charles, then that would give us evidence he was lying.'

Roddy was pleased to see a slight bloom coming to Mary's cheeks at the thought of being able to outsmart her uncle.

'Yes,' continued Donald. 'He couldn't deny Bert's story then.'

'Would you try to see him while I'm in Helensburgh, Roddy? He might even know who Charles passed the child on to.'

Roddy was pleased he had a role in this quest to find Mary's sister.

'I shall do it first thing tomorrow, Mary. Don't you worry. With Donald and me on the case, we will get answers.'

She laughed and gave him a quick hug.

'Right, let's get going. I didn't think I would ever get a chance of riding on your motorbike again. I can't wait.'

She then turned to Donald, and Roddy couldn't help feeling envious as he took her in his arms.

'A couple of weeks at the coast is just what I need, although I'm feeling better already, Donald. Thank you, my love. Can I have my ring back? I'm so sorry I threw it at you.'

The next day Roddy visited the hospital first thing in the morning before he went into the office. He thought he might have a better chance of talking to Dr Lamont by going early. But even if he couldn't see him today, then he could make an appointment for later in the day or even another day. The hospital was dark and uninviting. Built in the 1800s from red sandstone, it looked exactly what it was, a hospital for lunatics, a terrible and much maligned part of society. Tall trees blocked the sun and caused the area to be shrouded in shadow, creating an aura of secrecy and unease.

He rang the bell, and a middle-aged woman wearing glasses opened the door.

'Good morning. How can I help you?'

'I was hoping to see Dr Lamont and thought I'd come early before he started his rounds.'

'Do you have an appointment?'

'No, I'm sorry I don't, but I'm really keen to see him if he could spare me a few minutes.'

'May I ask what it is regarding?'

He took one of his business cards from his pocket and handed it over. She looked at it and then at him. He used the same cover story he had used when he visited Cheadle Royal.

'I'm a solicitor and I'm trying to trace someone on behalf of a client. I believe Dr Lamont may have some relevant information that would help me.'

She asked him to wait and gestured to a chair, saying, 'Dr Lamont is a very busy man, but I'll check if he has a few minutes to spare for you.'

Roddy was nervous. Would the man agree to see him? He would need to be at his most charming to get the information he needed from him. It was a very delicate situation. No doctor would want to admit that he had bent the rules for a friend.

The woman returned and asked him to follow her.

'Dr Lamont can spare you five minutes, Mr Macdonald. Make the most of it,' she smiled.

CHAPTER SIXTY-TWO

As Donald watched Roddy and Mary leave, he wondered when Mary had been on Roddy's motorbike. Neither of them had ever mentioned it. As he looked after them, he felt a twinge of jealousy at the way she had her arms wrapped around his waist and was leaning into him. He chided himself for his thoughts. Mary would never be unfaithful to him, especially with his brother. But he had a chill when he thought about how close they had come to splitting up when he told her what he knew. Perhaps they weren't as solid as he thought. But all the more reason to find out the truth for her. She would never leave him if he could answer all the questions that troubled her.

So, that evening, Donald went along to the club where he'd met Sir Arthur and Charles Adams. He believed guests could rent a room for a brief stay, so he thought it would be the best place to find Charles if he were still in Glasgow. He rang the bell and the same young man who had met him the last time opened the door.

'How can I help you, sir?'

'Hello, I don't suppose you'll remember me, but I was here the other day and met Sir Arthur for lunch.'

'I remember you, sir, but I have nothing to show that you are meeting anyone tonight.'

'No, I'm not. But when I was here the other day, I met Charles Adams, who is my fiancé's uncle, and I wondered if he was still here. It's in connection with his niece, Mary.'

'I shall check, sir. If you wouldn't mind waiting here, I shall return shortly.'

He then shut the door in his face. What a place. He bet there were all sorts of MI5 and MI6 people living undercover lives and using establishments like this one. Everything was so discreet.

The door opened again, and the young man asked him to come in. He then took him through to the lounge where Charles was sitting, smoking a cigarette, and reading the newspaper. He put it aside, looked up as he approached, but he didn't get up.

188

Probably still annoyed at his refusal to accept the job he was offering.

'I'm told you want to speak to me about Mary. Have a seat. What's the problem?'

He didn't beat about the bush, but launched straight in.

'Mary has found out that you lied to her about Bunty's baby. You told her it was stillborn, but she now knows the child survived and that you arranged for it to be adopted.'

He was a very cool customer. He just kept smoking his cigarette and looking at him, no surprise showing on his face.

'And what is it Mary wants to know?'

'She wants to know what happened to her sister.'

He stubbed out his cigarette and got up from the couch.

'Why don't you ask your mother?'

'My mother? My mother's dead.'

'Oh yes, your birth mother, the half Indian whose father was my uncle. I didn't mean her. I meant Chrissie Macdonald.'

'What's Chrissie got to do with it?'

'It was her who adopted the child.'

'No! Heather is Chrissie and Roderick's child. She was pregnant, and she had Heather after my father died.'

'Did she? Did you see her having the child? If you recall, she went to stay in Helensburgh with her sister and came back with a child.'

Donald was finding it hard to breathe.

'You're lying. Why would Chrissie adopt your sister's child? Bunty caused her husband to die.'

'It's true. Chrissie was pregnant by Roderick, but she lost the child. She was losing you and your brother too and was finding it difficult to cope. She felt a baby would help her and I felt it was better having someone who wasn't a stranger adopting Bunty's child.'

'So, you lied to Mary to protect Chrissie.'

'Not just Chrissie, but Bunty and her child. The stigma of illegitimacy can have a devastating effect, as I'm sure you know.'

189

'Did my Aunt Morag know about this?'

'Yes. She registered the baby's birth in Helensburgh. There are no other records of Heather's birth, so she can never find out the truth. You would do well to leave things as they are. I'm sure you don't want to hurt Heather or Chrissie. You're too nice a man for that. Now, if you don't mind, I have a train to catch.'

He signalled to the concierge, who came over and escorted Donald out. All he could think about were his words to Mary that he would never lie to her or hold back the truth ever again. But how could he betray Chrissie and Heather? They were his family. He decided he needed to talk to Roddy straight away, but he was taking Mary to Helensburgh. His stomach was in knots as he thought about Mary being in the place where Heather's birth was registered. Would Morag inadvertently give the game away? He decided to go to Roddy's office first thing tomorrow, to tell him what he'd found out.

CHAPTER SIXTY-THREE

After speaking to Doctor Lamont, Roddy went to work pleased with what he had found out. Hopefully, Donald had been as successful in finding Charles Adams. He couldn't wait to see him and compare notes. The whole thing was quite exciting. His thoughts returned to Mary and their ride down to Helensburgh. It was as exhilarating as the time she had ridden behind him through the Lancashire lanes. Now that he was aware of his love for her, he was also aware of the attraction between them. No novice with women and how they behaved when they liked him, he recognised the signs in Mary by the way she looked at him and moved her body towards him. He felt guilty though and vowed that he would never take it any further or do anything to hurt Donald. It would be the worst betrayal. But they needed him now and he couldn't turn his back on his brother and Mary despite his feelings and the danger it posed. His calling card had got him in to see Dr Lamont and he was sure it would open other doors if required.

When he got to the office, Donald was sitting in the reception area waiting for him. His face was pale and drawn. Something awful must have happened. What on earth had Charles told him? As soon as Donald spotted him coming through the door, he stood up and rushed towards him.

'Roddy, we need to talk.'

'Of course, but can't it wait till later, at least until I can go for my lunch break?'

'No, it can't. What Charles told me is devastating. You must come now.'

The receptionist looked at the two brothers, clearly wondering what was going on. She had never met Donald, so didn't know he was Roddy's brother and probably thought he was a dissatisfied client.

'Is everything alright, Mr Macdonald?'

'Yes, Miss Melrose. This is my brother Donald, and he has some news to pass to me. Is there a room we could use?'

191

'Yes, room two is free for the next half hour, so you could use that.'

'Thank you.'

As soon as they were inside room two, Roddy turned on Donald.

'What on earth did Charles tell you, that it can't wait?'

'Heather is Bunty's daughter and Mary's sister.'

'Heather? Don't be ridiculous Donald. She's *my* sister.'

'She's not Roddy. Chrissie is the person who Charles gave Bunty's baby to. She went to Helensburgh so that she could pretend she had a baby and pass it off as her own.'

His mind was in a whirl. He'd always wondered why his mother had left him and Donald at such a difficult time. And she was so defensive when he had visited her last year and mentioned what it would be like for Heather if she found out she wasn't her mother. No wonder she'd been upset.

'What are we going to do, Roddy? We can't betray Chrissie and Heather. They're our family.'

'Chrissie's not *your* family, Donald. In fact, if you think about it, Bunty, Mary, and Heather have a greater claim on you than Chrissie and me. You're their blood relation.'

'What are you saying? You think my loyalties lie with them rather than with you and your mother. I love you Roddy and Chrissie is my mother in all but blood. I can't bear the thought of hurting her. Think how Heather will feel if we tell Mary. The way Mary is just now, I don't think she would consider the consequences for Heather. She's too hell bent on getting justice for Bunty.'

'I'm surprised Charles told you the truth, aren't you? Did you believe him?'

'Yes, although he said there was no evidence to support it. He arranged with the psychiatrist that he would take the baby and have it registered in Scotland. He gave the child to Chrissie and she and Morag registered Heather in Helensburgh as if she were Chrissie and Roderick's daughter.'

192

'So, we could keep quiet and not tell Mary the truth.'

'I suppose so. What did Dr Lamont say?'

'He said Charles asked him not to register the baby's birth at the asylum as the church would find it hard to place a child for adoption whose mother was mad.'

'So, is that what we shall tell Mary? I feel so bad holding back the truth from her. I promised her I never would again.'

'You need to decide what you want to tell Mary, but I'm going up to North Uist to see my mother. I need to know why she adopted Bunty's baby. The only reasonable explanation is because Heather is Johnny's daughter, I think.'

'Yes, she looks so like him. I think you're right.'

'She loves that girl like her own and it will break her if the truth comes out. And Heather. What would it do to her?'

'I know what it did to us, Roddy, and I wouldn't wish that on anyone else. I think we have no option but to keep this information from Mary. How I wish I'd never told her anything. I've opened a Pandora's box.'

193

CHAPTER SIXTY-FOUR

Mary enjoyed her time at the hotel in Helensburgh. What better way to settle her mind than to walk along the front, read books, and eat delicious food? It had worried her when she couldn't stop crying. The thing she feared most had come true. She wasn't psychotic like her mother, but she hadn't been able to cope with the stress of work and finding out about her half-sister. She wondered how Roddy and Donald had got on and whether they'd found out the information they needed to find her sister. However, she did her best not to brood, as Donald called it, and resolved to have a proper rest. They would reveal everything when she returned from Helensburgh.

Sometimes she walked with Morag or played with her two children, Marion and Michael. One day when they were out for a walk on their own, the subject of Chrissie came up in the conversation.

'What made you come here, Mary? Donald just said that you were a little depressed by your job and needed some time off to rest.'

'Well, it was his idea. He told me Aunt Chrissie had come here to help with her depression after Roderick died. It had helped her, so he was sure it would help me.'

'Aunt Chrissie?'

'Yes, that's what I used to call her when my mother and I lived in North Uist.'

'You're Bunty Hepworth's daughter?'

Her cheeks flushed when she saw the look of understanding on Morag's face.

'Yes. I'm sorry. I thought Donald had told you when he asked if I could stay. Would you rather I leave?'

'No, not at all. I'm just surprised, that's all. I didn't realise you were Donald's fiancé. I thought you were just a friend, especially when I saw you riding up with Roddy on his motorbike. It made me think you two were a couple.'

194

Her face burned this time. It was thrilling to wrap her arms around Roddy's waist once more and to feel their bodies moving in harmony to control the bike. She had grown to like him and he her, but she hoped they weren't giving the wrong impression.

'Oh no, we're just good friends.' As soon as the words left her mouth, she knew she sounded like a cliché.

'So, are you finding it helpful to be here? Do you feel easier in your mind? I know being here did Chrissie a power of good. It was here she had Heather, you know.'

'Was it? I don't think I knew that. But I've loved my time here so I can understand how it helped Chrissie. And I'm lucky to have such a lovely fiancé and future brother-in-law. They are on a quest to get the information I need to set my mind at rest.'

'I thought you were feeling stressed because of your work. Is there something else too?'

Seeing Mary hesitate, Morag told her she didn't need to tell her, but Mary couldn't see any reason not to tell her. She probably knew a lot about her mother already.

'I recently found out that my mother had a baby when she left North Uist and I'm trying to find out what happened to it. Roddy and Donald are contacting some people to find out what they know.'

She noticed Morag's body stiffen momentarily at her words and wondered why. Did Morag know something? Before she could ask her, Morag looked at her watch and increased her walking pace.

'I better be getting back. That husband of mine will wonder where I've got to. See you later, Mary.'

CHAPTER SIXTY-FIVE

When I saw Murdo coming up with the post, I approached him eagerly, wondering who it was from. As usual, he could tell me.

'There's a letter from Morag for you, Chrissie. Didn't you get one just last week from her?'

'Yes, I did, Murdo, but it's always a pleasure receiving a letter from my sister.'

Morag's letter was much shorter than usual and looked as if she had written it in a hurry. I wondered why she had written to me so soon after her last letter. She must have something important to tell me. I felt a little quiver of excitement. What could it be?

Dear Chrissie

How are you, Heather, Mother and Father? I hope you are all well. Michael, the children, and I are well. The hotel is very popular, so we are busy too, but when Donald phoned to ask if his friend could come and stay for a week, I didn't like to refuse. He mentioned she was upset and depressed and he remembered that when you were like that, after Roderick died, you came here. He thought it might work the same magic on his friend. Luckily, it looks like being here is helping her, as she seems more cheerful than when she arrived.

It turns out she is actually Donald's fiancé, Mary, although I didn't realise that until I was out walking with her today. She arrived on the back of Roddy's motorbike, and I must admit; I was a little shocked at the brazen way she had her arms round him as she rode pillion. It's not a very ladylike way to travel. And how they looked at each other made me assume she was Roddy's girlfriend. I think she has your two boys wrapped round her little finger, as they are on a quest to find out information for her. Apparently, her mother had a baby when she left the island and Mary wants to know what happened to it. Good luck to them with that. It won't be easy, I'm sure, after all these years.

Take care

Your loving sister

Morag

PS She has asked me whether we do weddings? I thought they were being married in Lochmaddy. Have they changed their minds?

When I read Morag's letter, I wasn't happy at all and hoped Murdo hadn't sneaked a peek at the contents. Although, even if he had, there was nothing to show that I had any involvement in the matter of Bunty's baby. He would just think Morag wanted to give me a bit of gossip. But I wondered what was going on and what information my two boys were on a quest to find. What would they do if they found out the truth? It also surprised me at the comments Morag had made about Mary and Roddy. Did they have feelings for each other and didn't realise it? That would explain his outburst against Donald the day he found out he and Mary were to be married. What a mess?

I went to find my mother to let her know what Morag had told me, but stupidly left the letter lying on the table. When I came in from the barn, Heather had arrived home from school and had the letter in her hand. My heart sank, as it was obvious she had read it.

'I see you've read the letter from Auntie Morag. It's a shame that Mary hasn't been well, isn't it?

'Yes. I hope she gets better soon.'

She hesitated, then continued.

'Who is Mary's mother? Do I know her?'

A deep sadness enveloped me as I looked at my little girl. Was I doing the right thing, keeping the truth from her? Didn't she deserve to know who her birth mother was?

'No, you don't know her *mo graidh*. She lived here before you were born.'

'If she had a baby, why doesn't it live with Mary and her mother?'

'Och, it's complicated, Heather. Her mother was ill when she had the baby and couldn't look after her. So, her brother got someone else to look after the baby, but he didn't tell Mary.'

'She had a little girl, just like you.'

197

'Yes.'

'Well, it was nice for the baby that someone else took her. What a shame not to have your own *mamaidh* to look after you.'

Her eyes misted with tears, and I put my arms out for her to come to me. She came over and clung to me for a few minutes, obviously feeling distressed at the thought of not having a mother. The feel of her warm little body in my arms reminded me of how I had felt when Charles placed her in my arms all those years ago. The same feeling of maternal love for her overwhelmed me, and I vowed once more to do everything in my power to keep her safe.

After Heather had gone to bed, I asked my mother and father what I should do. They had no straight answer for me.

'You could tell Heather the truth, Chrissie,' said my mother.

'But you didn't see how she reacted today when she read the letter. She was so upset to think of the baby not having its mother. I just don't know how she would be if she found out she was that baby.'

'What about telling Roddy and Donald the truth and asking them to keep your secret?' asked my father. 'They love Heather and wouldn't want to do anything to harm her.'

'I know that's true, but I think they are both in love with Mary and that kind of love can surpass family love.'

'How can they both be in love with her? Donald is marrying her next month.'

'I know *Mathair*, but you read Morag's letter. She thought Mary and Roddy were a couple before she realised she was Donald's fiancé. And I remember how unreasonable Roddy was when he heard that Donald and Mary were getting married. I'm sure now he was jealous.'

'Look, I'm not feeling great, so I'm going up to bed. But my advice is to sleep on it and decide tomorrow. There's nothing you can do tonight,' said my father. He was right, but I doubted I would get much sleep.

CHAPTER SIXTY-SIX

When Mary arrived back from Helensburgh, she was feeling much better and was looking forward to hearing what Donald and Roddy had found out. But first she had to face Sister MacFarlane. Her face grew pink when she thought of what a fool of herself she had made.

'It's good to see you back, Mary. Tell me how you are.'

'I'm much better, Sister. I'm sorry for letting you down.'

'Yes, it's unfortunate, as it will be on your record. But then you're getting married and I assume you won't be doing much nursing. You'll be wanting to look after your husband and start a family, I expect.'

Mary's stomach clenched. What did Sister mean?

'It was my intention to look for a job in nursing, Sister. I know some professions don't allow women to work after they're married, but I believe nursing is different, isn't it?'

'I'm just wondering if you have the temperament for it, Mary. I've noticed you've been quite distressed occasionally during your training. Perhaps it's not the right vocation for you.'

'But I love it, Sister. I've never wanted to do anything else. Are you saying I've failed the course?'

'No, I'm not saying that. You've passed all your exams and have performed well in most of your duties, so it's not to do with your competence.'

'Are you worried that I'm too emotionally unstable to be a nurse?'

'Please don't upset yourself, Mary. That has had no influence on what I'm telling you. I shall give you a positive report, but I can't omit what happened last week from it. It would be wrong of me.'

'Okay Sister. I'll remember what you've told me and thank you again for your support last week. What will happen now? Can I return to duty until the end of term?'

'I don't think it would be a good idea for you to go back to the Royal, but I wonder if you could help in Men's Surgical until your course ends. You've worked there before, haven't you, and there were no problems?'

She nodded, cringing at Sister MacFarlane's words.

'It would be most helpful if you could do the back shift today. Nurse Sweeney has gone off sick.'

Mary had mixed feelings. Sister MacFarlane's request to work on the ward delighted her, as she felt sure she was being told in a roundabout way that she was no longer fit to be a nurse. But she was also desperate to meet Donald and Roddy to find out what they'd discovered. She would just have to be patient. Even if they had found out where her sister was, she could do nothing until she had finished her course. As she got ready to go on shift, for the first time, she realised her whole life was about to change. She would become Donald's wife and would no longer be living in the nurses' home. She would be free.

But something was wrong, and she wasn't sure what it was. Amid her fall out with Donald, she had received a letter from her mother telling her she was coming home for their wedding so she wasn't sure if that's what was wrong. The old nervousness she used to feel around her mother had resurfaced as she read the letter. It would be impossible for the wedding to be held in North Uist now. Too many terrible memories for her mother. She had sounded Morag out about having the wedding at her hotel and she had said they could do it. It was a lovely place and there was a Church of Scotland there too. She would need to ask Donald when she saw him.

CHAPTER SIXTY-SEVEN

It didn't take me long to decide what I was going to do as God set up an event that made it easy for me to meet up with Donald and Roddy the next day. As a result, I decided I would tell them the truth and throw myself on their mercy. The day following our conversation about Morag's letter and what to do about Heather; I was first up despite a sleepless night. I was surprised as normally my father rose at first light and there was no sign of him. I soon found out why when my mother came down shortly after me, looking worried.

'Your *Athair's* not well, Chrissie. I think we shall have to get the doctor.'

Getting a doctor was difficult. We would need to go to the post office and send a telegram and then, depending on where the doctor was and the weather, it could be hours before he could be here. Before I had time to ask what was wrong, there was a terrible cry from the bedroom. Mother and I ran upstairs.

'What is it, Angus? What's wrong?' she cried.

My father could not respond, but he didn't need to. His contorted face and the way he gripped his side told us the amount of pain he was in. This was more than just a sore stomach and I felt fear grip me. What if we couldn't reach the doctor? What if the doctor couldn't do anything for him, even if we did reach him? I was frozen to the spot, watching as my father broke into a cold sweat and cried out in pain. My mother was saying something, but I couldn't respond. My head was fuzzy with fear.

'Chrissie, didn't you hear me?' she shouted, and that cleared my head. 'You better get a message to Dr MacLeod right away.'

By this time Heather was up and standing white-faced, watching her grandfather writhing in pain.

'What's wrong with *Seanair?*' she asked, her lips trembling anxiously.

'I don't know, *mo graidh.* But let's get our bikes, and ride down to the post office so that they can deliver a telegram to the doctor.'

She did as she was told without saying a word, something unusual for her.

The post office was just opening by the time we got there. We threw our bikes down and rushed in, startling Fin, who was setting up for the day.

'Hello Chrissie. What are you doing here? It's not your day to be in, is it?'

'No Fin, it isn't. It's my father.'

I felt a lump in my throat and thought I was going to cry, but told him what was wrong without embarrassing myself. He was my boss, after all.

'My father is seriously ill, and we need to get the doctor to have a look at him as soon as we can. Can you send a message or are we quicker cycling over ourselves?'

'Well, he's not long after picking up some messages, so I can tell you where he was going, and you could cycle out to get him if you like.'

'Yes. We'll do that. Thank you.'

It wasn't too long before we caught up with the doctor, who was just getting into his car when we rode up on our bikes.

'Doctor, doctor,' cried Heather. 'You need to come and see my *Seanair*. He's very ill.'

'Alright, lassie, calm down now and let your *mamaidh* tell me what's wrong.'

I explained to him that my father had a terrible pain in his side, and he immediately diagnosed appendicitis.

'We will need to get him to hospital as soon as possible, Chrissie. He will need to be operated on right away.'

'But the hospital here doesn't do operations, does it, Dr MacLeod?'

'No, that's why I'm going to send for the air ambulance to take him to Glasgow. Take this message back to Mr Simpson at the post office and pack a bag for you and your father. I'll see to my other patients and then come and collect you both. We'll meet the aeroplane at Clachan.'

202

'I didn't know there was such a service. We've always had to take people by boat before if they needed hospital treatment.'

'It's new Chrissie. It was first used to take a man from Islay with stomach problems. The government has at last seen the sense of using aeroplanes for remote communities like ours. It'll save many islanders' lives, Chrissie.'

I was sure it would, but how I wished I didn't need to go up in the aeroplane. I felt sick at the thought. Birds flew, not humans. But when I remembered my father's cries, I knew I would need to do it if he was to be saved.

As I mounted my bike to go back to the post office, I looked at the note he had given me for Fin. It was addressed to the St Andrew's Ambulance Association and said, *Please send a plane. Urgent case of appendicitis.*

'Let's hurry Heather. Mr Simpson needs to send a telegram so that your *seanair* can go to the hospital.'

I'll never forget that morning. I packed a bag for my father and me and then we all sat looking out the window, waiting for the doctor to arrive. But the first person to arrive was Murdo, who pulled up in the van he delivered the post in. The doctor and the district nurse arrived a few minutes later. They lifted my father onto a stretcher and put him in Murdo's van. I went in the car with Dr McLeod. When we reached Clachan, there was an aeroplane sitting waiting for us. It had two sets of wings and its propellors were whirring noisily. The air was full of fumes from the engines, and I felt sick. The door was open and there was a small set of steps to climb in. Murdo and the doctor carried my father in first. I worried he would fall off the stretcher as they manoeuvred him up the set of steps and in through the small door space.

'Right, Chrissie. In you get. Nurse will go with you. There will be an ambulance waiting at Renfrew that will take you to the hospital in Glasgow.'

'Okay doctor. Thank you.'

Inside, the pilot was sitting in what is called the cockpit. I'm not sure why. It looked a bit cramped to me, with its buttons and dials and the handlebars for him to drive it. I felt dizzy at the thought of going up in the air and hoped the pilot was good at flying. There was a bench for my father to lie on, plus another bench for the nurse and me to sit on. It was bright inside, as there were windows all around and the sun had come out. Suddenly, there was a roaring sound, and we were moving. I gripped my father's hand, more for my comfort than his, and my stomach flipped as we left the ground. The nurse was so excited to be flying and kept pointing out the fluffy clouds and the scenery far below. But the roar of the engine and the bumping and bouncing about terrified me. I had to close my eyes when we were landing, as I was sure we were going to crash the closer and closer we got to the ground. But that flight saved my father. It was touch and go, but amazingly, we were in time for them to remove his appendix before peritonitis set in.

I waited in the reception area while they operated on him and then they allowed me in to see him when they took him back to the ward. He was very drowsy, and the nurse in charge told me I should go home and come back the next day. But where should I go? I hadn't thought to send a telegram to Katie or the boys. As I gathered my things together, I noticed Mary. I was surprisingly pleased to see her.

'Hello Auntie Chrissie. You look a little lost. Is your father alright.'

'He's still drowsy from the anaesthetic, so they've told me to go home and come back tomorrow. But I'm not sure where to go. In all the panic of my father being sick and us coming to Glasgow, I forgot to send a telegram to my aunt.

'Look, Donald doesn't live far from here, and I'm sure he'll put you up. I'll take you round as I haven't seen him since I came back from Helensburgh and am eager to hear his news.'

I was eager to hear his news as well and wondered how I could speak to him and Roddy before they spoke to Mary. As we walked, she chatted. But my mind wasn't taking in all that she was saying. I was so busy trying to figure out how I could delay her talking to the boys. Until she spoke about the wedding.

'I'm thinking we should have the wedding in Helensburgh, Chrissie. I know we said we would be married in Lochmaddy, but I've received a letter from my mother telling me she's coming home for our wedding.'

Bunty was coming to the wedding. This was the worst news. If Donald and Roddy had discovered the truth and told Mary, then she was bound to tell her mother. What if Bunty wanted Heather? Although it was a terrible thing to do, I secretly wished things weren't going well between Mary and Donald and that their wedding would be called off. I wouldn't need to see Bunty then. When we reached Mr Thompson's house, Roddy and Donald were there. Their faces fell when they saw me.

'Ma, what are you doing here?' asked Donald.

'I'm hoping you can give me a bed for a few days, Donald. Your grandad needed to be rushed to Glasgow on an aeroplane to have an operation.'

'An aeroplane!' said Roddy. 'How exciting.'

'Frightening is how I would describe it. I'm dreading going back. It was so bumpy and the noise from the engine was terrifying. Flying is for birds, not humans.'

He laughed.

'Och Mother, you're just an old fuddy duddy. Is Grandad alright? Was the operation successful?'

'Yes, praise God.'

'Grandad will be a celebrity when he gets back home as he must be one of the first people on the island to be helped by the new air ambulance service.'

'Yes, it's a miraculous thing, but I hope after I get your grandfather home safely, I never need to go on it again. But enough about that just now. Mary has news for you, Donald, about the wedding.'

CHAPTER SIXTY-EIGHT

Donald's mind was racing. He couldn't believe his mother had turned up at the same time as Mary. He was frantically thinking of how to separate them so that he and Roddy could tell Mary the lie they had decided on. Then his mother said something about Mary having news for him about the wedding. His stomach knotted. What now? He went over to Mary and took her hands.

'What is it, Mary? Are you not well enough to go ahead with the wedding?'

'No, Donald. It's nothing like that. I had a lovely time in Helensburgh and feel back to full health. It's about where the wedding is to be held.'

'But I thought you wanted it to be in Lochmaddy.'

'I did, but a letter from my mother has arrived and she tells me she's planning to come home for our wedding.'

Donald's heart sank. This was the last news he was expecting. What if she guessed Heather was hers when she saw how like Johnny she was?

'I don't think she will want to go back to Lochmaddy, do you?'

'No, I don't suppose she will. Do you want to have it in Manchester then?'

'I'm thinking Helensburgh at your Aunt Morag's hotel. It's a lovely place and I'm sure it could accommodate your family and mine. And if not, there are other hotels in the area guests could stay in.'

'What do you think, Ma? It means Grandad will probably not come.'

'No, he probably won't, but we would need to check with Morag and Michael that they don't have bookings. If they do, you might have to put the date back to a quieter time in the season.'

'Morag seemed to think it would be okay, but I suppose I better get in touch just to confirm or perhaps you could do it, Donald. She is your aunt, after all.'

Donald's mind was still racing, and he didn't answer her.

'I'll telephone Morag from the office tomorrow,' said Roddy with a tinge of impatience. 'Now Donald, don't you think you should get Mary down the road if she's working tomorrow? You have lots to tell her, I'm sure, and I have lots to tell Mother.'

He knew immediately what Roddy was meaning and stood up. Mary seemed to understand too, as she stood up and put her coat on.

'Let's go Donald. I can't wait to hear your news.'

When they got outside, she immediately asked him what he and Roddy had found out. So, he told her the story that Dr Lamont had told Roddy.

'So, they were trying to cover up where the baby had been born so that the church would accept her for adoption.'

'Yes, there's such a stigma attached to people in asylums that people won't adopt children who have been born there.'

'But was Uncle Charles able to tell you who had adopted the baby?'

'No, I'm sorry Mary. He handed the child over to the church. There will be no records as adoption arrangements were informal and didn't need to be registered.'

'But maybe if we went to the church, someone would remember. Did he say which church?'

He and Roddy hadn't considered that Mary would want to do this. They had assumed she would just accept the situation and that it would be impossible to find the baby.

'Mary, darling. I can sense you're getting all wound up again about this. Even if someone at the church remembers something, it's unlikely they will tell you. And if you think about it, the little girl will be twelve by now and settled with the family. Perhaps she doesn't know she's adopted. Think what harm you might cause her and her family if you breenge in and tell her the truth about her birth.'

Mary was in tears, and he held her close, longing to kiss her and make everything better. He hated lying to her. Would telling her the truth make things better or worse? He couldn't decide.

Although knowing that Chrissie had adopted Heather might relieve her worries about what had happened to her sister, it might not. And even if it relieved her worries, she might tell her mother and what would her mother do with the knowledge. Bunty coming home complicated everything even more. He couldn't take the chance.

CHAPTER SIXTY-NINE

As soon as Donald and Mary left, Roddy and Chrissie spoke at the same time.

'I've got something to tell you, *Mathair*.'

'I need to talk to you Roddy.'

They looked at each other, hesitating, then he spoke first.

'I know the truth, *Mathair*.'

He noticed her glistening eyes but made a conscious decision not to show her any sympathy. She had a lot of explaining to do.

'What truth?'

'About Heather. I know she's Bunty's daughter and that Charles Hepworth gave her to you. I know you went away so you could pretend that she was yours.'

'Who told you?'

'Charles Hepworth, who's a spy for the government, by the way; a member of MI5. He offered Donald a job spying on his friends.'

He could see his mother was incredulous by the look on her face. She clearly wanted to ask what he was talking about, but she stuck to the subject in hand.

'I knew from Morag that you and Donald were trying to help Mary find out what happened to the baby her mother had. So, I decided it was time I told you the truth. I wasn't sure when or how I could do that, but my father getting ill and needing to be flown to Glasgow, has given me the opportunity. So, ask me anything you want.'

He paused, trying to keep his feelings in check. It was like that day at Maude's house where he had lost control. He had so many questions. So much rage inside.

'Why did you leave Donald and me so soon after *Athair* died? Why was getting Bunty's baby more important than us, than me?'

He knew he sounded like a jealous little boy, but that was how he felt right now. All the hurt he'd felt back then, all the feelings of abandonment and loneliness of living on the croft without his mother and father, rushed back. He wanted to hurt his mother as much as she had hurt him.

'That woman tried to destroy your family, and you were too blind to see it. Why on earth would you want to help her by adopting her child?'

'Oh Roddy, *mo graidh, mo leanabh*. I'm sorry I hurt you. I thought you would be alright with *Seanair* and *Seanmhair.* Please forgive me.'

The tears that had glistened in her eyes were now overflowing and she was grasping at his hands, begging for his forgiveness. He felt tears sting his eyes. She looked so vulnerable. Her life hadn't been easy, so what right did he have to judge her? She had only done what anyone would do. Protect her family. He took her in his arms and shushed her before he spoke again.

'I'm sorry *Mamaidh*. I know why you adopted Bunty's baby. It's because the child is Johnny's. She was family, and I know what family means to you. But why all the lies? Why didn't you tell me and Donald?'

'To protect Heather. I thought the fewer people who knew, the better. I never dreamed that Mary would come back into our lives and would marry Donald one day. I can see I was wrong. But now that you and Donald know, are you going to tell Mary? Is that what Donald's doing just now?'

'No. He's telling her some of what we found out, but not about you having Heather. You can rest easy in that regard.'

'Och Roddy. This is all such a worry and everyone is coming to the wedding. I'm dreading it. Do you think I should tell Heather the truth before someone else does?'

'No. I think your secret's safe. When Charles Hepworth told Donald that it was you who adopted Heather, he told him he should let sleeping dogs lie. So, I doubt he'll tell Bunty or Mary anything.'

The door opened and Donald walked in.

'I've told *Mathair* what we know, Donald.'

'I can see that from the tear stains on both your cheeks.'

'What about Mary? How did she react to what you told her?'

210

'She was upset, Roddy, and wanted to find the church that Charles had handed the baby over to. But fortunately, she let me persuade her not to and has agreed to give up looking for the child.'

'So, our secret's safe?'

'For the moment Ma, for the moment.'

1935

THE WEDDING

CHAPTER SEVENTY

Mary looked in the mirror; a full-length one attached to the door leading into the bathroom. She had excused herself after dinner, telling everyone she wanted to be fresh for the morning. But the truth of it was she couldn't bear the tension. Chrissie was clearly uncomfortable seeing her mother again. Donald couldn't look at her Uncle Charles, she couldn't look at Donald, and Roddy was trying hard to avoid everyone. She and Donald should have run away to Gretna as they had joked about. It would have made things much easier.

Her reflection showed a young woman ready for bed, but tomorrow she would be in her wedding dress. This should be the happiest time of her life, but it wasn't. She and Donald hadn't moved beyond the occasional passionate kiss, and she wondered what their lovemaking would be like tomorrow night. She should be excited, but she wasn't. She felt like running away, but hurting Donald like that was unthinkable. Although he had become stronger and more outgoing since they had met up again, she wasn't sure he was robust enough to be jilted. Was anyone?

There was a light knock on the door, and she wondered if it was her mother. When she opened it, however, it was someone else entirely. Someone she wasn't expecting, and her heart thumped in her chest when she saw him.

'Roddy, what are you doing here?'

She pulled him into the room quickly, worried that someone might see him. What a scandal that would cause. A bride being visited by her bridegroom's brother the night before the wedding.

'I'm sorry, Mary, but I had to see you. After what happened in Glasgow, I need to know that you still want to go through with the wedding.'

She thought back to last week and all she could feel was shame, although it had been one of the most thrilling nights of her life. She'd been sitting in her room reading when she heard a noise. It sounded like rain pitter pattering on her window, but when she looked, it was perfectly dry. Puzzled, she opened her window

214

and looked out. Standing in the courtyard was Roddy. He'd thrown some of the small pieces of gravel in the courtyard at her window. She immediately thought of Romeo and Juliet and blushed. Roddy was her fiancé's brother, not her lover. What on earth was he doing here?

'Mary, can you come out to play?' he called.

'Shh', she called back, eager to get him out of the way in case she got into trouble. She was already in Sister Tutor's bad books because of what had happened when she became upset after she and Donald had fallen out. She wasn't sure what to do, but she needed to do it quickly before anyone saw him.

'Climb in here,' she hissed, opening her ground floor room window wide to allow him to climb in. Although other trainee nurses regularly used their windows to see their boyfriends, she had never done it before. Donald would never have asked her to do such a thing. It was exciting, she realised, wondering if the caretakers would catch her. It was their job to monitor who was coming and going after the housekeeper left for the day. When he had climbed in, she made him sit on the bed and then asked.

'What's happened Roddy? Is something wrong with Donald?'

She knew Donald, Roddy, and some of their friends were all going out to the Union for a drink to celebrate Donald's upcoming nuptials.

'No, nothing's wrong with my brother. There's something wrong with me.'

She could smell alcohol on his breath and wondered if he was drunk. She didn't like drunk men and kept her distance.

'What's wrong with you Roddy? Have you had too much to drink?'

'I've only had one pint, but I suppose it's given me courage to come and talk to you tonight before it's too late.'

'Too late for what? What are you talking about, man?'

'Love. That's what I'm talking about. I'm in love with you, Mary Hepworth, much as I hate to admit it. And if I don't tell you now, you'll marry my brother next week and we'll never have the chance to be together.'

Roddy rose from the bed and moved towards her, and she didn't resist when he took her in his arms. She looked up into his eyes as he spoke again.

'Oh Mary, I've known I've loved you since I came back from Manchester and that's why I've been keeping out of your road. But after seeing you again and feeling your arms around me on our way to Helensburgh, I can't pretend any longer. I feel I shall go mad if I don't tell you how I feel and ask you how you feel about me. Am I being stupid? Have I misunderstood? Is there any hope for me?'

She answered by reaching her lips up to his. At first, his lips caressed hers lightly, then he cupped her face in his hands and looked deep into her eyes. 'I love you, Mary,' he said, then kissed her in a way Donald had never kissed her. It was the sweetest, yet most passionate, kiss, and her body ached for more than kisses. Before she let herself think about what she was doing, she pulled him down onto the bed and gave herself up to the inevitable outcome of this action.

As they undressed each other in a slow, gentle manner, her eyes locked in admiration and amazement at his beauty. She responded passionately as his fingers explored and awakened her body in a way that she had never dreamed possible. Until she realised it was Donald's face coming into her mind, Donald's arms and kisses she was thinking about as Roddy made love to her. When they had finished, she was at a loss about what to do or say. She had just made the biggest mistake of her life, but she couldn't bring herself to tell Roddy. He was looking at her with such love, it would have been just too cruel.

'Say something Mary.'

Roddy's voice brought her back to the present.

'Of course, I want to go through with the wedding, Roddy. Last week was a mistake. It's Donald I love. I don't know what came over me. Please don't tell him what we did. We can't hurt Donald like that. He doesn't deserve it.'

There were tears in Roddy's eyes as he gazed at her, full of disappointment.

'No, he doesn't,' he whispered. 'What we did last week meant nothing, then?'

She felt as if her heart were breaking as she looked at the anguish on his face and was finding it difficult to breathe.

'I can't say it meant nothing, Roddy, but it's Donald I love. I beg of you, please don't make this harder than it is.'

He nodded, tears spilling over his cheeks, and turned towards the door, leaving her alone and full of guilt.

CHAPTER SEVENTY-ONE

Donald wondered where Roddy had got to. He was sitting in the bar alone. Everyone else had made their excuses and gone to bed early. Under normal circumstances, he and Roddy would have sat and talked about old times and discussed speeches on the night before his wedding. But they were both holding this enormous secret and were avoiding not only talking to each other, but everyone else as well. He thought everything would be okay now that he and Roddy had spoken to Chrissie and reassured her that her secret was safe with them, but it wasn't. He felt guilty about lying to Mary and knew that if she ever found out he had covered up the truth, she would never forgive him. Perhaps she already knew. She'd been avoiding him since Bunty and Charles arrived in Glasgow.

When he thought about Charles Adams, his hackles went up. He despised the man. He wasn't a card-carrying Communist despite what Charles thought, but his request to spy on his friends almost converted him to their cause. It would have been easy, as Rosemary was an enthusiastic Communist, eager to share her beliefs and ideals. She had given him lots of pamphlets to read and last month had asked him if he would like to go to Spain with her.

'Things are changing over there, Donald, and I want to see it for myself. Why don't you come with me? A last adventure before you settle down to married life.'

He liked and admired Rosemary. Unused to receiving attention from women, he thought her interest in him was just political and an attempt to convert him to the cause. But her invitation made him wonder if she liked him in a more romantic way and he was a little uncomfortable. It would be unthinkable to go away with another woman when he was so soon to be married, even if it was innocent. So, he politely turned her down.

But apart from Mary avoiding him, something else was wrong. Since they had left Glasgow, Roddy hadn't said a word. He seemed a different man after the night last week in the Men's

218

Union, where they had gone with some friends for a drink. He hadn't wanted to go, but Roddy had insisted, so he gave in. To his surprise, Roddy only had one pint and seemed on pins most of the night, so Donald was relieved when he excused himself early, saying he wasn't feeling too good. But when they met the next day, he looked as if he had been out all night and Donald wondered if he had a secret girlfriend.

Roddy had never been the same since losing Theresa, and he felt sorry for him. He was the lucky one. Tomorrow he and Mary would become man and wife. He had always enjoyed their kisses but had never let it go any further than that. It wouldn't have been fair to her, even although he knew she would have liked him to be more passionate. He was inexperienced in the ways of women and was a little scared of what would happen tomorrow night. But he hoped his love for her would banish all his fears and she would be happy with his lovemaking.

Just then he spotted Roddy making his way out of the hotel and rose to go after him. When he went outside, he could see Roddy's head was down and he was muttering to himself and crying.

'Roddy!' he called. 'Is something wrong?'

'Everything's wrong Donald. Everything.'

He was about to follow him when he heard his mother calling him softly.

'Donald, come away in.'

'Something's wrong with Roddy, Ma. He was crying and muttering to himself.'

'I know, I saw him. Just let him be. Whatever's bothering him will sort itself out.'

He looked after Roddy and hoped his mother was right.

CHAPTER SEVENTY-TWO

Feeling bereft after his chat with Mary, Roddy walked along the front, its gaslit streetlamps twinkling prettily in the lapping waves as the sun set. What had he done? How would he ever be able to look Donald in the eye again? He'd betrayed him in the worst way. Why had he given into his feelings? He was just too impulsive. Thank God Donald hadn't followed him. The mood he was in, he would probably have selfishly confessed everything and the wedding would have been off. Even Donald wouldn't be able to forgive that betrayal. And Mary. His lovely, loyal Mary. She was now condemned to marry Donald, carrying a terrible secret. Why hadn't he left her alone? He was so caught up in his thoughts he didn't see the woman coming towards him and almost bumped into her.

'Roddy.'

He stared at her. Bunty. The woman who had harmed his family so much. His initial reaction was one of hatred. This woman had killed his father. She was the reason their lives were in such a mess. He had often wondered if he had it in him to kill anyone, and right now, he believed he could. His fists clenched as he stared at her with open hostility. She took a step backwards and a look of alarm crossed her face. As he glared down at her, he realised how frightening he must appear. To him, he was still a boy, and she was still his cruel teacher, but to her he was a man a full six inches taller than her, on the verge of violence. Oh God, what had he become? His father would be ashamed of him. He had hated the woman, that was true, but he would never have harmed her.

Mary's face came into his mind, and he remembered what she had told him about her mother. She had endured so much cruelty and heartbreak. No wonder she ended up in an asylum. She wasn't a monster; she was just a woman who had suffered. Just like his mother had suffered, just like he and Mary were suffering just now.

'Oh, I'm sorry to frighten you, Mrs Hepworth. I was so caught up in my thoughts, you startled me.'

'Are you okay Roddy? You look a little upset.'

'Och, it's just the wedding and everything. I'm thinking about my father and wishing he could be here,' he lied.

'So, it's not because you and Donald found out from my brother that your little sister is actually my child?'

'You know?'

'Charles told me what had happened with your brother. He felt I should know in case Donald went against his advice and told Mary. Did he tell Mary?'

'No. We weren't sure how she would react. What are you going to do now that you know? Will you tell Mary?'

'I don't know, Roddy. I need time to mull things over. It's such a lot to take in. I'll let you continue your walk now and I'll see you tomorrow.'

As she walked away, part of him hoped Bunty would tell Mary. He still couldn't fully believe that what had happened in Glasgow had meant nothing to her, despite what she said. So, if she was looking for a way out of marrying Donald, she had it. He had promised never to hold back the truth from her ever again, but he did. Because he felt so guilty about it, he would readily accept it was the reason Mary was calling off their wedding. He waited a little while and then walked back to the hotel, a glimmer of hope fluttering in his heart. If the wedding was called off, it was possible that in time he might have a chance with her. When he returned, it surprised him to see his mother and Bunty sitting in the lounge chatting. He would like to be a fly on the wall of that conversation.

CHAPTER SEVENTY-THREE

I was still standing outside, enjoying the evening air, when I spotted Bunty Hepworth walking up the path to the hotel. I almost sneaked back inside so that I wouldn't need to speak to her, but as I would need to speak to her sometime, it might as well be now. As she approached, she smiled tentatively at me, and my mind went back to those turbulent years she had spent in North Uist. I recalled the havoc she had created in our lives, culminating in Roderick dying and me having Heather. When I gazed at her, I was taken aback by the pang of sadness that washed over me as I remembered how close we had once been. But it was all just a pretence, and I could almost hear Roderick's voice warning me to watch out. She had fooled me before and could do so again.

'Hello Bunty. How are you after your long journey from Canada?'

'I'm well, Chrissie. I spent a few days in Manchester with my mother before travelling here, so I feel quite refreshed.'

'I hear you've settled in Canada and are teaching in the small town of Saltcoats close to where Roderick and I used to live.'

'Yes, that's right. Amelia and Aleksander Bukowski asked me to send their regards to you when they heard I was coming to Scotland.'

I shivered when she mentioned the Bukowski family. It was when they bought James Adams' vacant land and began to prepare it for cultivation that Bunty's father's body had been found. As if she had read my mind, she told me she had visited the land where they had found her father and had also visited his grave.

'I realise now how wrong I was to blame Roderick for my father's death. He would never have come back for my mother and me. I was delusional and was only trying to make sense of my anger at how my stepfather treated me.'

I gaze at her and sense a composure in her manner that was never there when she was young and hoped the troubled person she was back then had found some peace.

222

'You seem a different person from what you were all those years ago, Bunty. Did you receive help when you transferred to the asylum in Manchester?'

'No, far from it. No. I met a man through my job in Canada, and it was he who helped me the most.'

'Oh, I didn't realise you had married.'

She laughed.

'Not that kind of man, Chrissie. No, it was a doctor by the name of Samuel Laycock. He specialised in child psychology and set up the Home and School Association. It was through attending one of his talks that I met him.'

'What's the Home and School Association?'

'Dr Laycock believed it was important for teachers and parents to work together when children were misbehaving to find a solution. He believed if you could find out why children were engaging in destructive behaviour, you could help them change that behaviour. So, he set up the Association.'

I remembered how Roddy had been towards Donald when they were children and wished there had been something like that in Uist.

'And how did he help you?'

Her face flushed a little, and I realised it was something she might not wish to talk about.

'Sorry I'm being nosey. You don't need to tell me if you don't want to.'

'I don't mind. I suppose now that I'm to be your son's mother-in-law, you'll want to know that I'm no longer mad.'

It was my turn to flush with embarrassment.

'No, I didn't mean that.'

She laughed again.

'Don't worry Chrissie. I'm only teasing. Dr Laycock believed that childhood events caused mental ill-health. This was a liberating discovery for me. I can't tell you what a relief it was to realise that I hadn't just inherited a cruel gene, that I wasn't just my father's bitter seed. Dr Laycock worked with me to help me

223

understand how my unhappy childhood had affected my behaviour in adult life.'

'I'm pleased for you, Bunty.'

And I was pleased for her. She'd had a rotten deal in life and deserved some happiness. However, I decided we had shared enough this evening. I didn't want the conversation to stray on to the baby she had had with our Johnny, so I yawned.

'Well, I think I better be getting inside and go to bed. It's a big day tomorrow.'

'Goodnight Chrissie. Sleep well.'

CHAPTER SEVENTY-FOUR

Mary was still asleep when her mother knocked on her door. It had been the early hours of the morning before she'd fallen over, but she was now sound. For a blissful moment, she forgot what day it was as she surfaced from her slumber and then everything flooded back into her mind. It was her wedding day, but she was no longer a virgin, feeling nervous about her wedding night. Her nervousness was about whether Donald would find out she had been unfaithful to him before they were even married.

'Mary, I've brought you some tea and toast. I know you probably won't want to eat a full breakfast, but you need to have something. It will be a long day without some food in your stomach.'

'Thank you, Mummy.'

As she sipped her tea and nibbled the toast, she gazed at the white silk dress hanging at the front of the wardrobe. Was it only a few months ago she had picked that dress with such joy and hope for the future? She had been happy and looking forward to spending the rest of her life with Donald. Somehow, everything changed when she found out he had lied to her. But he wasn't the only one. Her uncle Charles, Roddy and even her grandma had lied. Yet she had let it affect only her feelings for Donald. It was partly the reason she'd let Roddy make love to her. He was handsome, and there was a definite spark between them. But she realised now by giving in to his advances, she was punishing Donald for his lie. What a fool she had been. She didn't deserve Donald and wondered if she should confess. But what good would it do? She couldn't betray Donald even more by abandoning him on their wedding day.

'Mary, I've got something I need to say to you. I know it's your wedding day, but I'm hoping what I'm about to tell you will settle your mind and you'll enter your marriage with a light and happy heart.'

Mary sighed. How she wished she could have a light and happy heart. She looked at her mother. What a different person she seemed to be from the woman who had gone to Canada all those years ago and who used to frighten her with her unpredictable behaviour.

'Okay, Mummy. What is it you wish to tell me?'

'Charles told me you have been a little upset in recent months because you found out I had a baby and you were worried about what had happened to the child. I know he lied to you, but he was only trying to protect my reputation and the reputation of our family.'

'So, you agreed to him taking your baby and having it adopted?'

'Yes, as much as I could agree to anything back then. I was quite ill.'

'I know. I was with you when you began talking to Johnny when he wasn't there, and when you sat in a scalding hot bath with a knife.'

She didn't mean to be cruel to her mother, but she couldn't stop the way her words came out. Why was she telling her all this today of all days?

'It must have been very hard for you, Mary. I am so sorry. But an illness of the mind is as debilitating and as beyond anyone's control as an illness of the body, but no one sees it. There's no bruising or bandages, only the loss of rational thought.'

She understood completely what her mother was saying. Hadn't she felt like that after finding out Donald had lied to her? She rose from the bed and walked towards her mother. How could she have ever been afraid of this woman? She'd always been the kindest of mothers to her, despite the suffering she had endured.

'I love you Mummy. I'm sorry for everything that's happened to you. Thank you for coming to Scotland for my wedding. It's so courageous of you. It must be hard facing Chrissie and her family again.'

'You are everything to me, Mary, and I would face the Devil if I needed to. But luckily Chrissie isn't the Devil. In fact, in some ways, she's an angel.'

'An angel? Why?'

'She's looked after my baby, your sister, for the last twelve years.'

'What do you mean? Charles told Donald he'd given the baby to the church for adoption.'

'No, he didn't. He gave Heather to Chrissie. She had miscarried her own child and was bereft at losing Roderick, so she needed something to live for. And that something was Heather.'

Mary couldn't quite take in all that her mother was telling her. Heather was her sister!

'But you mustn't tell her, as she doesn't know. I'm only telling you because I don't want you to be worrying about anything on your special day. Now let's get you ready. You'll make a most beautiful bride.'

She was in another world as her mother helped her do her hair, affix her veil, and put on her dress. Heather was her sister, and she was okay. Her mother had been right to tell her. It did give her peace of mind, knowing Chrissie had been looking after her little sister all these years. It would be difficult not to tell Heather what she knew, but she didn't want to cause her any distress. She would need to tell Donald, though. She didn't want to keep any more secrets from him than was necessary to protect their marriage.

As she wondered how he would take it, there was a light knock at the door. Her mother opened it and there stood her sister, looking as pretty as a picture.

'I'm ready, Mary. Do you like my dress? I'm so looking forward to being your bridesmaid.'

Mary smiled through her tears.

'You look beautiful, Heather. Thank you for walking with me today. When a girl doesn't have a sister, she needs a kind sister-in-law like yourself to help her on her wedding day.'

Heather stuck her tongue in her cheek and put her head down, looking as pleased as Punch.

'Right Heather, you come with me, darling. We'll give Mary a little time on her own and you can help me get ready. Is that okay?' We'll come and collect Mary when we're ready to go.'

'Okay, Mrs Hepworth.'

After her mother and Heather had gone, Mary sat on the chair at the window, looking out onto the courtyard. It was a beautiful, sunny day. Perfect wedding weather. She felt herself relaxing. Knowing that her sister was okay had lifted a heavy load from her shoulders. Marrying Donald was the right thing to do, despite what had happened with Roddy, so she would make the best of things and enjoy their wedding day. A knock on the door interrupted her thoughts, and she rose to open it, fully expecting to see her mother and Heather. But it wasn't them. It was Donald, in his wedding kilt and jacket. Her heart fluttered in her throat like a baby bird trying to fly. Why was Donald here? Had he discovered what had happened with Roddy?

CHAPTER SEVENTY-FIVE

Tears nipped Donald's eyes as he gazed at Mary. She was quite beautiful in her wedding frock. How he wished he would be the one to undress her tonight, make love to her, and become her husband. But he knew it was unlikely. When she found out he had lied to her again, he was certain she would call the wedding off.

'Oh Mary, you look so beautiful.'

He moved forward to take her hands, but she stepped back from him.

'What is it, Donald? Why are you here?'

'I can't go through with the wedding, Mary.'

He noticed a look of fear cross her eyes and wondered if maybe he was wrong. Maybe she loved him so much, she would forgive him.

'Why not, Donald?' Her voice was a whisper. 'Is it because of Roddy?'

'Roddy? No. Why would I call off our wedding because of Roddy?'

He was finding it difficult to understand why she would say this. What had Roddy got to do with things? But he'd been off with him since last week. Had something happened that he didn't know about?'

'What is it, then?'

He swallowed and nibbled on the nail of his little finger.

'I haven't been completely honest with you, Mary. I can't go into our marriage, breaking the vow I made to you never to lie to you or keep back the truth from you ever again. It would make a sham of the vows I will say in front of the Minister today.'

'I think I know what you didn't tell me, Donald.'

'You do? How?'

Her eyes filled with tears and she took both his hands in hers.

'My mother came to see me this morning, and she told me your mother was the person who adopted Heather. She told me so that I could relax and enjoy my wedding day. And I can't explain, but I feel so much better knowing that my sister has been in safe hands all these years.'

His heart filled with hope. Was she saying she would still marry him?

'So, you forgive me for not telling you the whole truth?'

'I do, Donald.'

'And you'll still marry me today?'

'I will, Donald.'

Taking her in his arms, he kissed her more passionately than he had in a long time. He was overwhelmed with love and desire for her and didn't hold himself in check, as he had been doing over the last couple of years. He could sense Mary's surprise at the urgency of his kisses, and it was she who drew back.

'Let's wait till tonight, Donald,' she whispered. 'We've held ourselves back all this time. Besides, you might crumple my dress.'

She smiled at him with sparkling eyes.

'I love you so much, Mary Hepworth. When I promise to love and cherish you today, I will mean it with all my heart. Thank you, my darling, for being so understanding. I better get going. I can't have the bride arriving before the bridegroom.'

He was halfway through the door when he remembered what she'd said about Roddy and turned back.

'What did you mean when you said was Roddy the reason I couldn't go ahead with the wedding?'

He saw the look of fear cross her eyes again and knew there was something she wasn't telling him. But did he really want to know? He recalled how upset Roddy was last night. Was he in love with Mary?

'I feel there's something else you're not telling me, Mary. I can see it in your eyes. What are you afraid of?'

He could see her swallow. Something was obviously worrying her. He heard a noise behind him and turned to see Roddy. What was he doing outside Mary's room?

'She's afraid you'll find out that I'm in love with her.'

230

So, he'd been right. Roddy was in love with her. But why did Mary look so scared? Did she feel the same about Roddy, but couldn't bring herself to tell him?

Mary's eyes were blinking wildly now, and she put her hand to her throat.

'I didn't mean for it to happen, Donald. It just did.'

'What did Mary? What happened?'

'I told Mary how I felt about her last week. You remember when I left the Union early? That's where I went.'

He looked in disbelief at his brother. His world was crumbling around him. Everything he thought was true was a lie. His brother had betrayed him. But did Mary love Roddy? Had the woman he had loved all his life betrayed him, too? His ears were buzzing, and he couldn't think straight. More than anything, he wanted to punch Roddy, and felt his fingers close into a fist. Then he remembered that brute, Patrick Dunlop, and loosened his fingers. He would never stoop to such behaviour, no matter how much Roddy had hurt him.

'There's no need to look so upset, Donald. Mary turned me down point blank. She told me it was you she loved, and you she intended to marry.'

'Is it true, Mary? Is it me you love?'

Tears were streaming from her eyes now, and she glanced at Roddy before turning to him.

'Yes Donald. It's you. I don't feel about Roddy the way I do about you. I didn't tell you what Roddy had said, as I knew you would be upset. I'm sorry. Please forgive me.'

Relief swept over him. She loved him. She was going to marry him.

'There's nothing to forgive, my sweetheart. You were only trying to protect me.'

He had almost forgotten Roddy was there, and it startled him when he heard his voice.

'Do you still want me to be your Best Man?'

231

He hesitated. Did he? This man, who he called brother, had sneaked behind his back to steal Mary from him. It was unforgivable. Yet everything that had happened now made sense. Roddy had been in love with Mary for the last few years. That's why he'd distanced himself from them. He was trying to protect them. But when he and Mary had asked for his help, they had forced him into their lives again. It was because of them he had been tempted to declare his love. He could understand why. Mary was adorable. He wasn't sure how things would go between Roddy and him in the future, but for today, he would put his anger at him aside. The wedding was going ahead and Roddy would be part of it.

'Yes. You're lucky I didn't punch you; you know. But I'm glad you've told me the truth. Now, let's get going. Everyone will wonder where we are.'

As the two of them left, Bunty and Heather were approaching and looked puzzled at the sight of the two brothers leaving Mary's room. Luckily, there was no time for them to offer an explanation.

CHAPTER SEVENTY-SIX

Helensburgh, Scotland, 1935

Before I can make a fool of myself by raising the alarm that Bunty has run off with my daughter, the sound of the organ swells, and I hear urgent footsteps running down the aisle. It's Roddy and Donald, and they stand in front of the minister, both trying to catch their breath. Then Bunty appears and sits down beside me. I breathe a sigh of relief and turn round to see Mary on the arm of Charles, with Heather behind them. Mary is wearing a beautiful full length white satin dress with a veil that Heather is carrying in her white-gloved hands. Heather looks so proud and smiles widely at us as she walks behind Mary. In fact, she looks so much happier than Mary, with her pale face and puffy eyes, that I wonder if Donald and Mary are doing the right thing.

As Mary reaches the front of the church, Bunty turns and whispers something I can't hear.

'Sorry, what did you say?'

'I know what you did,' she says, a little louder, a smile playing on her lips.

Silence descends as the wedding ceremony begins, so I don't have time to respond. But I can't concentrate on the service. All I can think about is Bunty and what she'll do now that she knows Heather is her daughter. Will she want to take her away from me? Could she take her away from me? That was something I hadn't thought to ask Roddy. He could have advised me now that he's almost a qualified solicitor. Even if that's not what she intends to do, will she tell Heather the truth? When I think about it, everyone in the family now knows about Heather and perhaps it's time for her to know, too. I can't let my daughter's happiness and wellbeing be left to chance. Look how keeping Donald's birth a secret affected our family. I wonder who told Bunty and whether Mary knows as well. Perhaps that's why there was a delay in the wedding party arriving. I pray Heather hasn't heard anything to make her suspicious.

233

When it's all over, we gather outside. There are cars waiting to take us back to the hotel. My head's pounding and my neck is tight with tension. I need to ask Bunty what she meant. Perhaps she's talking about something else entirely and it's only my fear making me think she knows the truth. When I notice she's taking Heather into a car with her, I decide to act. I couldn't bear it if she told Heather she's her mother when I'm not there.

'Bunty, can I talk to you for a minute before you go?'

She smiles at me and nods, and we move away from the car and Heather.

'What did you mean when you said you knew what I'd done?'

'You know what I meant, Chrissie, but you don't need to worry. I'm not about to reveal your secret. You did me a huge kindness that I can never repay. Thank you.'

Her eyes glisten with unshed tears, and she squeezes my hand.

'Would you and Heather like to join my mother and me in this car?'

I nod gratefully, but my heart misses a beat when Heather speaks to Bunty on the journey back to the hotel.

'You're the lady who couldn't look after her baby and she had to be adopted, aren't you? It's so sad that you never got to bring her up.'

I hold my breath, waiting to hear how Bunty will answer her.

'It is Heather. But do you know something? I bet whoever adopted my little girl is the best mummy in the world and takes good care of her.'

I look at Bunty, hoping she knows how grateful I am. She's keeping my secret safe, but is that the right thing to do? Perhaps we should both tell Heather the truth and then there will be no more secrets, no more lies for people to find out, and no more lives to be destroyed.

When we arrive back, the staff hurry us into the dining room for the wedding meal. Because of the delay in the service getting underway, they are on tenterhooks to get us seated, and the food

234

served. There's plenty of wine for the speeches and the toasts and then the dancing begins. Perhaps it's just me, but I feel the atmosphere is lighter than it was yesterday. Everyone seemed tense, and I worried things would not go well. But here we are all dancing, chatting, laughing, and enjoying ourselves. During a break in the dancing, Mary and Donald come and ask if they can speak to me privately. We go outside and sit on a bench in the courtyard. The sun is shining, the bees hum as they gather nectar from the roses and a refreshing breeze blows from the sea. A sense of wellbeing envelopes me and I realise I'm not worried by what they're about to tell me.

'There's something you need to know, Ma.'

'I think I know already, but tell me, anyway.'

'Mary, my wife,' he says, smiling proudly down at her, 'and her mother both know the truth about Heather. Neither of them will tell her, so you no longer need to worry, Ma. Your secret's safe.'

'I can't tell you what a relief it's been for me, Auntie Chrissie, to know that you've had Heather all this time. When I found out my mother had a child and that she'd been adopted, it worried me so much that the family who adopted her may have treated her unkindly.'

'I understand Mary. It was one reason I asked your Uncle Charles if I could adopt Heather. She's Johnny's daughter, my niece, and part of our family, after all. I couldn't bear to think of her being looked after by strangers.'

We all hugged, then Donald said they had something else to tell me.

'Mary and I have decided to go back to Canada with Bunty. Mary wants to spend more time with her mother, and I want to find out more about my mother's family. I hope you're not disappointed with our decision.'

'Och Donald, I'll miss you, of course I will. But you and Mary must do what's best for you. No matter where in the world you are, you'll always be my son.'

His eyes fill with tears.

'And you'll always be my Ma.'

He hugs me again and then asks.

'What about Heather? Will you tell her the truth now?'

'I think I will, but I'm not sure when. I know how much hurt it caused you, and I would do anything to save Heather from the suffering you went through.'

'I know you'll do what's best for Heather, Ma. Anyway, Mary, shall we go in and have our last dance? I don't know about you, but the honeymoon suite Morag has given us looks very comfortable.'

I swear he winked at her, and pray all will go better for them on their wedding night than mine did with Roderick. We'd spent it apart and had not consummated our marriage until almost three weeks after we married. I remember the hairbrush he gave me that night. It still sits on my dressing table and sometimes Heather brushes my hair with it, not knowing what pleasure she gives me by doing so. I sigh, wishing again that Roderick was here to share in the celebration.

'You look miles away, *Mathair,*' says Roddy, interrupting my thoughts.

'I was thinking about your *athair* and wishing he was here with us.'

He nods.

'I hope you're okay today, Roddy. You were very upset last night. Donald wanted to follow you, but I told him not to. Did I do the right thing?'

'Yes, *Mathair*, you did. I would probably have said something I would have regretted. And I would rather do anything than hurt my brother.'

'He tells me he and Mary are going back to Canada with Bunty. I think it'll be good for Donald to see where he was born and find out more about his mother's ancestors, don't you?'

'Yes, I do.'

'And it'll be good for you not to have to see Mary?'

He smiles.

236

'How do you know so much, *Mathair*? I think you must have some of the second sight that the islanders speak of.'

'Not second sight, Roddy, just overwhelming love for my son and his wellbeing.'

He smiles and takes my hand.

'Right *Mathair* of mine, let's dance.'

So, I dance. I know I'll need to decide when to tell Heather the truth, but it doesn't need to be tonight. It's something to think about tomorrow, when the wedding is over, and we go back home to North Uist.

The End

Curious to know what happens to Chrissie and her family?
Buy the next book in the series by clicking on the QR Code.

ACKNOWLEDGEMENTS

I enjoyed writing this third book in The Uist Girl Series. I wanted to move on to the younger members of the Macdonald family and thought the fact there were two boys and one girl lent itself to a love triangle. The book takes place mostly in Glasgow this time, my hometown, so it has been easier for me to write about the setting. North Uist still features, of course, but to a lesser extent. The inter-war years are an interesting period in history, so I enjoyed the research I did for this book.

Some things I write about are based on stories my mum told me about her young days in the thirties. Dancing with Benny Lynch was one of them. My husband also has a walking stick belonging to his grandfather, which is engraved to show that he walked in the 1936 Hunger March. So that's why I have included the Hunger Marches in the story. The little bit about the Means Test at the front of the book comes mostly from the BBC Bitesize Series.

Details of the Scottish Hunger March to Edinburgh I got from *Three Days that Shook Edinburgh,* written by Harry McShane.

To find out more about nursing during this period, I read *A Nurse in Time* by Evelyn Prentis. It was very informative and I've used it to describe Mary's experience as a nursing trainee.

Glasgow University Library was very helpful and pointed me toward places to help with my research. One of these was archive copies of the Gilmorehill Globe, which gave me an insight into student life at that time.

Through various websites on Google, I found out quite a lot about the political and economic situation and mental health treatments of the period.

In my previous research, I found out that Native Canadians had fought in the First World War and Henry Norwest was one of the most famous.

An article written by Dr A J MacLeod about the first air ambulance service for the Western Isles, I found on the internet too. The first air ambulance apparently landed at a cairn at Clachan on North Uist in 1933.

I would like to thank the following special people in my life for their help and support. I couldn't do it without them.

My readers, Liz, Margaret, Elizabeth, and Ian. Thank you for reading and making comments. I appreciate the time you give to this and for your constructive and helpful comments.

My sister, Catherine, for her enthusiastic encouragement and commentary on my manuscripts.

My husband's cousin, Joan Somers, who kindly copy-edited my book.

My husband, Charlie, for his continued support, which has been unfailing since I began writing. He's a superstar.

Finally, thank you for buying my book. It would really help other readers to decide whether to buy it if you left a review on Amazon or Goodreads. Thank you.

ABOUT THE AUTHOR

Marion Macdonald is a Scottish novelist who lives in Glasgow with her husband, Charlie. She developed an interest in creative writing when she retired from her job as Director of a Housing Association and enrolled on a course with the Open University in 2015.

She wrote and self-published her first novel, One Year, in 2017. It was runner-up in the Scottish Association of Writers' Competition for a self-published novel in 2020. Since then, she has written and self-published a further six novels.

Marion was born and educated in Scotland and has an Honours Degree in English Literature and History from the University of Glasgow.

Scan the QR Code if you wish to join her reader newsletter group. When you sign up, you will receive a free copy of Wherever You Go, a compilation of her short stories and poetry.

OTHER BOOKS BY THIS AUTHOR

THE EWAN AND SUZIE SERIES

THE UIST GIRL SERIES

The QR Code will take you to my Amazon Author Page where you can buy my books.

Printed in Great Britain
by Amazon